The Cupcake Diaries

Mia's
Baker's Dozen

Coco Simon

SIMON AND SCHUSTER

First published in Great Britain in 2013 by Simon and Schuster UK Ltd
A CBS COMPANY

Originally published in the USA in 2012 by Simon Spotlight, an imprint of Simon
& Schuster Children's Division, New York.

Simon & Schuster UK Ltd
1ˢᵗ Floor, 222 Gray's Inn Road, London WC1X 8HB

Simon & Schuster Australia, Sydney
Simon & Schuster India, New Delhi

A CIP catalogue record for this book is available from the British Library.

ISBN 978-0-85707-885-8

1 3 5 7 9 10 8 6 4 2

Printed and bound in Great Britain.

www.simonandschuster.co.uk
www.simonandschuster.com.au

CHAPTER 1

I'll Definitely Finish It Tomorrow . . .

Me llamo Mia, y me gusta hornear pastelitos.

That means "My name is Mia, and I like to bake cupcakes" in Spanish. A few months ago, I could never have read that sentence or even written it. Maybe that doesn't sound like a big deal. But for me, it totally was.

Here's the thing: I'm good at a bunch of things, like playing football and drawing and decorating cupcakes. Nobody ever *expected* me to be good at them. I just was.

But everyone expected me to be good at Spanish. My whole family is Latino, and my mum and dad both speak Spanish. I've been hearing it since I was a baby, and I can understand a lot of it and speak it pretty well – enough to get my point across. But reading and writing Spanish? That's a whole other thing. And the fact that I was bad at it got me into a big mess. Well, maybe I got myself into a big mess. But Spanish definitely didn't help.

The whole situation kind of blew up this winter. You see, when I started middle school in the autumn, they placed me in Advanced Spanish with Señora Delgado because my parents told the school that I was a Spanish speaker. At first I did okay, but after a few weeks it was pretty clear to me that I was in over my head. I could speak it but not write it. The homework kept getting harder and harder, and my test grades were slipping.

One night in February, I was trying really hard to do my Spanish homework. Señora asked us to write an essay about something we planned to do this month. I decided to write about going to see my dad, who lives in Manhattan. I visit him every other weekend, and we always go out to eat sushi.

It sounds simple, but I was having a hard time writing it. I always get mixed up with the verbs, and that was the whole point of the essay – to use future indicative verbs. (Yeah, I'm not sure what those are either.) Anyway, I was trying to write "We will eat sushi," and I couldn't get the verb right.

"*Comemos*? Or is it *comeramos*?" I wondered aloud with a frown while tapping my pencil on my desk. My head was starting to really hurt, and it wasn't just because of the homework.

"Dan, TURN IT DOWN!" I yelled at the wall in front of me. On the other side of the wall, Dan, my stepbrother, was blasting music like he always does. He listens to metal or something, and it sounds like a werewolf screaming in a thunderstorm. He couldn't hear me, so I started banging on the walls.

The music got a little bit softer, and Dan yelled, "Chill, Mia!"

"Thanks," I muttered, even though I knew he couldn't hear me.

I looked back down at my paper, which was only half finished. Where was I again? Oh, right. Sushi. At least that word is the same in any language.

My brain couldn't take any more. I picked up my smartphone and messaged three of my friends at once.

Anyone NOT want to do homework right now?
I asked.

Alexis replied first. She's the fastest texter in the Cupcake Club.

Mine is already done!

Of course, I should have known. Alexis is one of those people who actually likes doing homework.

It's better than babysitting my little brother! came the next reply.

That's my friend Emma. I actually think her little brother, Jake, is kind of cute, but I also know that he can be annoying.

The last reply came from my friend Katie.

Let's go on a homework strike!

I laughed. Katie is really funny, and she also feels the same way I do about a lot of things (like homework). That's probably why she's my best friend here in Maple Grove.

Where are we meeting tomorrow? I asked.

I think I mentioned the Cupcake Club already. That's a business I started with Alexis, Emma and

Katie. We bake cupcakes for parties and other events, and we meet at least once a week.

We can do it at my house, Emma replied.
Works for me! Alexis texted back at light speed.

Alexis always likes going to Emma's house, and it's not just because she and Emma are best friends. She used to have a crush on Emma's brother Matt. He's pretty cute, but Emma's brother Sam is even cuter.
Alexis texted again.

Everyone come with ideas for the Valentine's cupcakes.
Ugh! I hate Valentine's Day! Emma complained.
But there's CHOCOLATE! Katie wrote.
And everything's pink, I reminded Emma since pink is her favourite colour.
K, you have a point. But still. We have to watch all the couples in school make a big deal out of it, Emma replied.
And watch all the boys go gaga for Sydney, Alexis chimed in.

Sydney is the president of the Popular Girls Club, and Alexis is right – lots of boys like her.

Any boys who like Sydney have cupcakes for brains, Katie wrote.

I laughed.

Got to go! Twelve more maths problems left! Emma wrote.

I have 2 go study, Alexis added.

I thought you were done? Katie wrote.

This is just for fun ☺ , Alexis wrote back.

If u want to have fun u can do my homework, Katie typed.

Or mine, I added.

LOL! CU tom, Alexis typed.

I said good night to my friends and put down my phone. I stared at my paper for a few seconds and then I picked up my sketchbook.

My Spanish class isn't until after lunch, so I figured I could finish the essay then. I couldn't concentrate now anyway. Besides, I was dying to finish a sketch I had started earlier.

My mum's a fashion stylist, and she's always taking the train to New York to meet with designers and boutique owners. I guess I take after her because I am totally obsessed with fashion and I love designing my own clothes.

6

Once in a while, Mum takes me to meetings with her and I get to see all the latest fashions before other people do.

Lately I've been trying to design a winter coat that keeps you warm but isn't all puffy. I hate puffy coats. I thought maybe the coat could be lined with a fabric that kept you warm *and* looked streamlined. Maybe cashmere? But that would be really expensive. Flannel might work; and it would be so cozy, like being wrapped up in your bed's flannel sheets!

I opened up my sketchbook, a new one that my dad gave me. It's got this soft leather cover and really good paper inside that makes my drawings look even better. I picked up a purple pencil and started to finish my sketch of a knee-length wraparound style coat.

There was a knock on my door, and then Mum stepped in.

"Hey, sweetie," she said. She nodded to the sketchbook. "Done with your homework?"

"Yes," I lied.

Mum smiled and walked over to look at my sketch. "Very nice, *mija*," she said. "I like the shape of those sleeves. And purple is a very nice colour for a winter coat. Most winter coats are black or brown or tan. They're so boring."

"Thanks!" I replied, and she kissed me on the head and left the room. I started to feel a little guilty about lying about my homework, but I pushed the feeling aside. I was definitely going to finish it tomorrow, so no problem, right?

Actually, it *was* a problem . . . a big one.

CHAPTER 2

Señora Is Not Happy

I know how to say all the colours," Katie said helpfully. "Red is *rojo*. Blue is *azul*. Yellow is *amarillo*. I'm not so good at pronouncing that one because I can't do that thing with the two *l*'s."

It was lunchtime, and I was frantically trying to finish my essay while eating the chicken salad sandwich that Eddie, my stepdad, had made for me.

"Thanks, Katie," I said. "But I don't think the colours will help. I need future indicative verbs."

Katie frowned. "That sounds painful. But maybe you could, you know, pad it. Like say the sushi restaurant has red chairs and a blue rug and yellow walls."

I laughed. "Can you imagine if a restaurant was really decorated like that?"

"Rainbow sushi!" Katie exclaimed. "I think it would catch on."

I sighed. "Anyway, I need verbs."

Alexis and Emma walked up to the table carrying trays of spaghetti and salad. Alexis nodded at my notebook.

"Cupcake ideas?" she asked.

"I wish," I replied. "It's my Spanish homework."

Alexis's green eyes widened in horror. "You mean you didn't finish it?" Most people have nightmares about monsters, but Alexis wakes up screaming if she dreams she hasn't done her homework.

"It's hard!" I complained. "I'm supposed to be writing about when I go see my dad. Now I'm trying to say, 'We will visit my grandmother.'"

Alexis frowned. "We haven't done a lot of future tense in our French class yet. Spanish must be a lot harder than French."

I shook my head. "It's because I'm in Advanced Spanish," I said with a moan. "That's why we're already on this."

"But you speak Spanish, Mia," Alexis said. "I've heard you!"

"Yes," I replied. "But I've never taken a Spanish class. I took French in my old school. And when we moved here, my mum thought I should get some formal training in Spanish. She told the guidance counselor that I spoke Spanish at home, and they put me in the advanced class. Without even asking me!"

"So it's not easier because you already speak it?" Katie asked.

"No way," I said. "It's like, when I hear people talking in Spanish, I can understand most of it. And if someone asks me a question, like my *abuela*, I can answer her. But my main language growing up was English."

I took a sip of my water. "And think about it," I said. "You learned how to speak English before you could learn how to properly write it, right? You can say to a baby, 'Show me your nose,' and the baby will point to her nose. But she isn't able to write, 'My nose is on my face.'"

Katie nodded. "You're right," she said. "I can see why it's more difficult to learn how to write a language than to speak it."

I picked up my sandwich, and Katie eyed it. "Did Eddie make you chicken salad again?"

"Uh-huh," I answered, taking a bite.

"He's a really good cook, isn't he?" she asked.

"His chicken salad's pretty good," I admitted.

11

"But believe me, you do not want to eat his Mystery Meat Loaf."

Katie looked thoughtful. "Maybe he can be my top chef when I open up Katie's Rainbow Restaurant," she said.

"Ooh, that's a great idea," Emma said. "You could divide the menu into seven colours, and people could pick one food from each colour."

"That's way too much food," Alexis objected.

"Well, you wouldn't have to order *all* seven," Katie pointed out. "You could order three dishes of your favourite colour, if you want."

Did I tell you that my Maple Grove friends are a little bit crazy? They always make me laugh. Maybe "creative" is a better word than "crazy" to describe them. Everybody always has lots of ideas. A rainbow restaurant! Only one of my friends would dream up something like that.

When I look at our lunch table, I sometimes think we are like a rainbow of hair colours. Emma's hair is pale blonde, the colour most women in Manhattan pay a fortune to try to get. Alexis has gorgeous, curly red hair. Katie's hair is light brown and wavy, and mine is black and really straight.

"We could all be waitresses," I suggested. "We could each wear a different colour uniform."

"I'll be violet!" Katie cried. She loves purple.

Emma frowned. "There's no pink in a rainbow."

"You could be red," Alexis suggested.

"Red is *so* not pink," Emma protested.

"I'll be red," I said. Then I took out my sketchbook and started drawing our uniforms.

Before I knew it, the bell rang. Lunch was over, my assignment wasn't done — and I had to go to Spanish class.

"Wish me luck," I said.

"Everybody forgets their homework at least once," Katie said, trying to cheer me up. "It'll be okay."

The problem was, I hadn't forgotten to do it — I just *couldn't* do it. There's a big difference. If you forget to do your homework, it's a one-time thing. But if you don't know how to do it, it's a huge problem. And I didn't expect things to get easier.

I gathered my books together and headed to Señora Delgado's class. The only good thing about that class is that I sit next to Callie, who's pretty nice. She used to be Katie's best friend, but that's kind of a long story. And she hangs out with Sydney and is in the Popular Girls Club. And Sydney doesn't really like me, but that's another long story.

Anyway, I like Callie, and it's nice sitting next to her in class. Especially when things get confusing. She's really helpful.

Callie gave me a smile when I slid into the seat next to her.

"Nice shirt," she said, admiring my boxy blue knit shirt. I had accessorised it with a necklace one of my mum's designer friends had given me – a silver chain with a chunky silver circle pendant.

"Thanks," I said. "I like your scarf." Callie was wearing one of those loopy big infinity scarves in red and black that looked nice with her black jumper.

"Thanks," she said back.

Callie is into fashion too. That's one of the reasons we get along. But our little mutual admiration session was the highlight of my Spanish class.

"Hola, clase," Señora Delgado said when she walked into the room. That means "Hello, class." In advanced class we're supposed to speak Spanish all the time, which is pretty easy for me. (But since you might not speak Spanish, I'll do all the dialogue in this class in English.)

Señora began by asking us each to say a few sentences about what we did the day before. That's so we could practise our past tense. I was able to do that okay.

"I did my homework, talked to my friends, and drew in my sketchbook," I told her, and Señora smiled.

"Perfect pronunciation and accent as usual, Mia," she said. "Good job."

But Señora wasn't smiling at me after she asked us to hand in our assignments. I handed it in and held my breath. Señora went through the pile of papers and then frowned.

"Mia, this is only half finished," she said.

"I know," I said. "I'm sorry."

Señora shook her head. "You are getting lazy these days, Mia. This is not acceptable. See me after class. I'm giving you an extra worksheet for homework tonight."

"Yes, Señora," I said.

Callie gave me a sympathetic look, and I slunk down in my seat. This was just what I needed. More homework that I didn't understand.

I know what you're probably thinking right now. Why didn't I just tell my parents the truth? That I shouldn't be in Advanced Spanish.

Well, I just felt like I couldn't. What would they think? The truth was that their only child,

Mia Vélaz-Cruz, the daughter of proud Spanish-speaking parents, couldn't read or write the language. I didn't think they could handle the truth. It would have to be my secret. Hopefully they would never find out.

CHAPTER 3

Sweet and Spicy

$\mathcal{A}$t least I didn't have to face Mum right after school because we had an official Cupcake Club meeting. Emma lives close to the school, on the same street as Alexis, so the four of us walked to her house. It was cold out, and there was still some snow on the lawns from a storm the week before. My red winter jacket kept me nice and warm, though, and for once I didn't mind its general puffiness.

When we got inside, Mrs Taylor was sitting at the dining room table with Emma's little brother, Jake. He was taking the books out of his backpack.

"Hi, Mum!" Emma called out. "Did you get off early?"

"I'm working story time tomorrow morning, so I had the afternoon off," her mum replied. She's a librarian, and she's got blonde hair just like Emma and all her brothers.

Jake ran up to us. "Are you making cupcakes today?" he asked. "I want a blue one with a dinosaur on it!"

"Sorry, Jake, today we're just talking about cupcakes," Emma told him. "But maybe you can help me make some later, okay?"

Jake got a big smile on his face. "Okay!" Then he ran back to the table.

"There's a pot of hot chocolate on the stove, and some cereal bars to go with it," Mrs Taylor said.

"Thank you!" all four of us said at once. Then we headed to the kitchen for our meeting.

You can tell from Emma's kitchen that everyone in her family loves sports. There are sports schedules tacked to the refrigerator, and her brothers' hockey sticks were leaning up next to the back door. The one thing of Emma's that stands out is her pink mixer. Besides being gorgeous, it's great for baking cupcakes.

"Emma, we should use your pink mixer to make our Valentine's cupcakes," Katie suggested as we grabbed our cocoa and snacks. "Maybe they'll add some extra Valentine's magic or something."

Alexis opened up her backpack and took out her notebook.

"So, the bookstore wants four dozen cupcakes for their event," she said, getting right down to business as usual. "And they want them to be Valentine-themed. Any ideas?"

"I was thinking we could do a white cupcake," Emma said. "You know, the kind you make with no egg yolks? They're fluffy and light as air. I think they're called angel's food."

Katie nodded. "My mum showed me how to make those." (Katie's mum is, like, the best cupcake baker in the world.)

"And then we could make some light pink strawberry frosting to go with them," Emma finished.

We all made an *ooh* sound.

"That sounds so pretty!" I said. "I had a different kind of idea. I was thinking about something red – maybe a red velvet cupcake, but with red cinnamon frosting and spicy sweets on the top."

"Spicy romance!" Katie said, and we all laughed.

And that was exactly when Emma's brother Sam walked in. How embarrassing!

"Spicy romance?" he repeated. "What are you girls talking about? I thought this was a cupcake meeting."

Sam is in high school, and his blond hair is wavy and sometimes falls over his eyes. And he's just as nice as he is cute.

"This *is* a cupcake meeting," Emma said with a huff. "We're trying to invent some Valentine's cupcakes."

Emma's brother Matt walked in just behind Sam. He opened the refrigerator, took out a carton of milk, and drank right from it.

"Valentine's cupcakes?" he asked. "What, for your boyfriends?"

"We're too young to have boyfriends!" Katie blurted out. "At least, that's what my mum says."

Matt shrugged. "Well, then you can make some for me to give to my girlfriend."

Next to me, Alexis suddenly got a weird look on her face.

"You don't *have* a girlfriend," Emma said. "And stop drinking from the milk carton or I'll tell Mum!"

Matt reached over her shoulder and grabbed

two oatmeal bars from the plate on the table. "Well, maybe I'll get one," he said.

Emma shook her head. "Exactly. You don't have one."

Most of the time, Emma is pretty quiet and shy. But when she's with her brothers, she can totally stand up to them. I think that's cool.

Alexis's face was all pink underneath her freckles. I know she used to like Matt (and maybe she still did, a little), so it must be weird to hear him talking about girlfriends.

Sam took the milk from Matt and poured himself a glass.

"There's too much spicy romance in this room," he said. "I'm getting out of here."

Now it was Katie's turn to blush, only she turned as red as the cupcake I was imagining.

"Can we please get back to our meeting?" Alexis asked impatiently.

"We have two cupcake ideas," I reminded her. "Fluffy and pink, and red and hot."

"We should do both," Katie suggested. "One pink, one red. Sweet and spicy."

"Good idea," Alexis said. "Then people will have a choice."

I started sketching a big heart entirely made of

cupcakes. All the pink ones were in the middle, and the border was made with the spicy red cupcakes. "Here's a fun way to display them," I said. I held up my sketch.

"I love it, Mia!" Emma squealed. Nothing like a big pink heart to make a girlie girl happy.

"That's awesome," Alexis said. "Now we have two cupcake ideas and even a cool way to display them. This was a very productive meeting." She nodded approvingly.

"That was easy!" Katie said, leaning back.

Alexis stood up. "I'd love to stay longer, but I think I should go home," she said.

"Already?" Katie asked.

She nodded. "Tons of homework."

"I think teachers get bored in the winter and give us extra homework so they have something to do at night," Katie mused. "It seems like it's double lately."

Suddenly I remembered the extra homework Señora Delgado had given me.

"I should go soon too," I said. "Let me text Eddie."

"My mum can give you a lift," Katie said.

"That's okay," I told her. "He's expecting me to text him to pick me up."

My stepdad, Eddie, is a pretty nice guy. I don't have too many complaints about him, even though it's superweird that my parents are divorced and I have a stepdad in the first place. But one thing that bugs me is that he's way more strict than my dad, and Mum goes along with it.

For example, Mum works at home on her business, but she's out at meetings a lot. And she and Eddie have a rule that I can't be home alone. So if Mum's not home, then Eddie leaves his office, which is here in Maple Grove, and hangs out with me until Mum comes home.

Can you believe that? I mean, I'm in middle school! Emma's mum lets her stay home alone, and she even watches Jake. It's so not fair. When I'm in Manhattan with my dad, sometimes he'll run out to the shop or something and *he* lets me stay in the apartment by myself. But not Eddie. And I know Mum's only going along with it because that's what Eddie wants.

I hung out with the Cupcake Club for about fifteen more minutes, and then Eddie called my phone. He doesn't believe in beeping the horn. He says it "disturbs the peace."

I said goodbye to my friends and headed outside. Eddie's car was nice and warm.

"Hi, Mia," he said cheerfully. "How did the cupcake meeting go?"

"Good," I replied. Eddie always wants to have these long, chatty conversations, but sometimes I'm not in the mood.

"Do you have a lot of homework tonight?" he asked as we began the drive home.

"Um, some," I said. There was absolutely no way I was going to tell him what happened in Señora Delgado's class.

"You can start that while I start dinner then," he said. "And don't forget to text your mum as soon as we get home."

"Why do I always have to do that?" I asked. "*You* know I'm home! Why do I have to tell both of you?"

Eddie laughed. "Because your mum likes to hear from you."

I rolled my eyes and stared out the window. Back when Mum and Dad were still together, I had a babysitter who picked me up from school when they were both working late. Her name was Natalie, and she was really nice. She would make me mac and cheese for dinner, and I was usually in bed when Mum came home and kissed me good night. Mum never made me text her then.

But there was no use arguing with Eddie. I texted Mum as soon as I got home, and she said she'd be home by six thirty. Then I decided to text my dad to see if he wanted to Skype. Thinking about those old days in the city was making me miss him really bad.

In a meeting. We'll Skype after dinner, OK? he texted back.

K, I answered, feeling a little sad.

"Guess it's just me and Eddie," I muttered.

There was nothing to do but start my homework. I did my maths first and then my vocabulary, and then I started on my Spanish.

Soon a delicious smell filled the air, and I realised that Eddie was making his famous spinach lasagna for dinner. *Yum!*

When I heard the door slam, I knew Dan was home. A little while later, my mum pulled into the driveway.

"I hope I'm not late!" Mom called out.

I ran down the stairs, remembering I should have set the table by now. But when I got into the dining room, Dan was already setting it.

"Hey, thanks," I said.

Dan shrugged. "Dad said you were doing homework."

Eddie walked into the dining room carrying a steaming pan of lasagna. He was wearing my mum's oven mitts with the big red roses on them, and he looked pretty silly.

"Let Family Time begin!" he announced in a goofy voice.

A few minutes later I was eating delicious lasagna and salad and garlic bread, and Mum was telling me about her new client, and then Dan told this story about this guy in his chemistry class who made something explode, and we were all laughing. It was definitely better than eating mac and cheese with Natalie. In fact, it was pretty nice.

But you know what would be even better than that? Having "Family Time" with me and Mum and Dad all together. It doesn't really feel like "Family Time" to me completely without my dad here eating dinner with us. But that's never going to happen again.

And sometimes knowing that really hurts.

CHAPTER 4

Thank Goodness for Cupcakes

I felt a little better after I Skyped with my dad; I always do. And I definitely didn't want to disappoint Señora Delgado again, so I made sure I finished all my homework. They were both worksheets, so I ended up guessing a lot. But at least I finished!

Anyway, tomorrow is Friday, which is my favourite day of the week. For one thing, it's the last day before the weekend, and the best things always happen on weekends. But for the Cupcake Club, it's also Cupcake Friday.

We started Cupcake Friday when school started and we all met. I definitely wouldn't mind eating cupcakes every day, but that's not exactly healthy, you know? So every Friday one of us brings in cupcakes to share. Since we started our business, a lot of times the cupcakes are test runs of the cupcakes we're going to make for an order.

The next day in the cafeteria, we all waited eagerly for Emma to arrive. Last night Emma texted everyone and told us she was going to bake the white cupcakes with strawberry frosting. She came to the table with a pink cardboard box and lifted the lid.

"They're a little messy, because I let Jake help me," she said apologetically. "So I added some coconut flakes to cover up the dents in the icing."

"That looks like snow!" I said. I took my sketchbook out of my bag and started sketching with a pink pencil. "I like how it looks on top, but maybe we could test out some other decorations too. Like some white heart-shaped sprinkles, maybe?" I held up my sketch.

Emma's eyes lit up. "Ooh, I like that idea!"

Katie picked up a cupcake. "They look sooo good, Emma," she said, peeling off the wrapper.

We hadn't even eaten our lunch yet, but none of us could resist trying one. I unwrapped one and took a bite. The white cake was superlight and fluffy, and the strawberry icing was perfect – not too sweet.

"It's almost like eating a cloud," Katie remarked, finishing her cupcake in one big bite.

"It is delicious," I agreed.

"It's perfect," Alexis added. "Now we just need to test the spicy ones. Mia, can we do that at the meeting on Sunday?"

"Oh, I almost forgot!" I said. "My friend Ava is coming out to visit this weekend. Is it okay if she's at the meeting?"

"She's nice," Katie said. "Besides, since we're making cupcakes for her birthday party, she can tell us what she wants."

"She's the one we met at your mum's fashion show and wedding, right?" Alexis asked, and I nodded.

"Of course she can be there," Alexis said. She looked down at her notebook. "Oh yeah, I forgot something. I meant to mention this yesterday."

I smiled. "Yeah, it looked like you were a little distracted."

Alexis blushed. "I told you, I don't like Matt anymore! Besides, you and Katie turn bright red whenever Sam walks into the room."

"Ew! You guys are talking about my brothers, remember?" Emma pointed out.

"Sorry," I said. "So what's up, Alexis?"

"The question should really be, 'What's down?'" Alexis said. "And the answer to that would be 'our sales.' They've dropped twelve percent since the fall. We had a little bump during the holidays, but still, we need to pick up business."

"Maybe we can start promoting the business again," Emma suggested. "Remember when we handed out those flyers? They really worked."

Alexis nodded thoughtfully. "True. We haven't done those in a while. But maybe we could put a coupon on them or something. You know, like a special deal."

"We could do a baker's dozen!" Katie said.

"What's that?" Alexis asked.

"It's when you buy a dozen of something and you get an extra for free," Katie explained. "Like they do at the bagel shop. They give you thirteen bagels for the price of twelve, and they call it a baker's dozen."

"I like it!" Alexis said. "Except for one thing. Our cupcake boxes fit twelve cupcakes exactly. Where would we put the extra one?"

Everyone was quiet for a minute. "Maybe we could wrap the extra one in a clear bag with a ribbon," I said. "Then they'd definitely see that they're getting an extra one."

"So cute!" Emma agreed.

"They also make special boxes that fit exactly one cupcake," Katie said. "I've seen them at the store. But they might be too expensive. I can check."

"Either one of those ideas could work," Alexis said. "And you know, maybe we don't have to do flyers. I was doing some research on advertising, and it costs only ten dollars to put an ad on the school's website for parents. Since we need some new customers, we could offer a baker's dozen to everyone who orders for the first time."

"Sounds like a plan!" Katie said.

"I can write something up and show it to you guys on Sunday," Alexis said.

"And I'll get the ingredients together for the cinnamon cupcakes," I added.

And then I realised that I had spent the whole lunch hour without even thinking about Spanish class. That's another reason I love being in the Cupcake Club!

CHAPTER 5

Some Advice from Ava

Why exactly do I have to sweep the basement?" I complained. "Nobody ever goes down there!"

"Would you take a bath and not wash your feet?" Eddie replied. "A truly clean house is clean all over. And we want things to be nice for your friend."

"But she's not even going to see the basement!" I pointed out.

That was when Mum stepped into the kitchen. "Mia, please don't argue with Eddie. It will only take a few minutes to sweep the basement."

I glared at my mum, but I knew I wasn't going to win this argument. So I grabbed the broom from Eddie and went down the stairs.

"No stomping!" Mum called after me.

"I am *not* stomping!" I called back. (Although to be honest, I was stepping pretty hard.)

I couldn't help it. I was feeling pretty cranky. Ava was due any minute, and I was thinking of changing out of my skinny jeans and black jumper into something different. But no – I had to clean the basement.

When we lived in an apartment, we didn't have a basement. In fact, I don't remember cleaning our apartment. I had to keep my room clean, but the kitchen and living room were always neat. I never thought much about how that happened.

But now I lived in a house, and Eddie believes that "a clean house is a happy house." So every Saturday we wake up at the crack of dawn (which to me is any time before ten o'clock) and clean the house, unless I have a football game or a cupcake job. It's just one more way that my new life is worse than my old life.

Even though I hate to admit it, Mum was right about the basement. There's not much down there except Dan's and my sports equipment and a metal shelf with some pots and pans and cans of food. The floor is concrete, and it didn't take long to sweep at all.

But by the time I got back upstairs, the doorbell

was ringing. My heart started to beat extra fast. Ava was here!

Ava and I have known each other since nursery school. She was my only best friend in the world until I met Katie. I miss Ava so much! I usually visit her when I spend the weekend with my dad, but she's never been to Eddie's house before – I mean, *my* house. Our house.

I ran to the door and opened it. Ava was there with her mum, Mrs Monroe. A blast of cold air swept into the room.

"Come in, fast!" I said. "It's cold out there."

Then Mum and Eddie came up, and everybody hugged one another. Ava took off her coat, and I saw she was wearing skinny jeans and a black jumper – just like me.

We pointed at each other and laughed.

"Nice outfit," I said.

"You too," Ava replied.

I've always thought that Ava and I look kind of alike, even though I'm Latina and she's part Korean and part Scottish. We're both the same height, and we both have brown eyes and straight black hair. Oh, and we both have first names that are three letters long. How cool is that?

Eddie took Ava's purple duffel bag from

Mrs Monroe and brought it over to the stairs.

"Ellie, can you stay for coffee?" my mum asked Ava's mum.

"I wish I could, but I've got to get back for Christopher's hockey game," Mrs Monroe replied. She hugged Ava and kissed her on the forehead.

"Call me if you need anything, okay? Otherwise I'll see you at the train station tomorrow."

"Okay, Mum," Ava replied.

When Mrs Monroe left, Eddie said, "Mia, why don't you give your friend a tour of the house?"

"Um, sure," I said. I felt a little awkward. I'd never had to give Ava a "tour" of anything. But everything was different now.

"I'll take you on the grand tour!" I said dramatically, and we both started giggling. "Follow me, madam."

So I showed Ava the kitchen and the dining room, and she kept saying, "Wow! You have so much space!" It's true, I guess. In Manhattan, almost everyone I know has a pretty small apartment.

When we got to the living room, Dan was setting up his video game system.

"Oh, hey, guys," he said, nodding to Ava. "You were at the wedding, right?"

"Right," Ava said, and I saw her cheeks turn pink.

"Ava, you remember my stepbrother, Dan," I said.

Dan nodded and settled down in front of the TV. Then I led Ava upstairs.

"Your brother is so cute!" she whispered when we got to the top.

"He's not cute! He's just . . . regular," I said. Suddenly I knew how Emma must feel with everyone crushing on Matt and Sam. "Besides, he's not my brother. He's my stepbrother."

"Oh yeah, I forgot," Ava said as I opened the door to my room. Then she gasped. "Wow, look at all this space!"

I had been nervous about showing Ava my bedroom. My room in Manhattan has this cool Parisian theme, and it's light pink and black and white. But I haven't decorated my room in this house yet. Right now it has ugly flowered wallpaper on it, but Eddie promised to scrape all that off for me. I still haven't figured out what colour to paint it, and none of the furniture matches.

But Ava didn't seem to notice. She went straight for my closet and threw open the door. "Oh wow! This is HUGE!" she exclaimed. "You could fit a whole store in here, Mia!"

My closet isn't really *that* big, but compared to my old one in the city, it definitely is huge. Then Ava frowned.

"Wait! I can't find anything!" she cried. "Where's my favorite top? The one with the butterfly? It used to be next to the red dress!"

"I reorganised it," I told her. "Mum showed me how to do it by colour. Look in the blue section."

Ava searched and then pulled out the shirt. She held it in front of her. "You have to let me borrow this again! When it gets warmer, I mean."

"Or you could layer it," I said. I rummaged through the clothes and pulled out a slim-fitting, long-sleeved knit top with purple-and-blue stripes. "See?"

"Cool!" Ava said, grabbing it from me. "Can I borrow them both? I'll give them back next time I see you."

"Of course!" I told her. "You don't even have to ask."

Ava flopped backwards on my bed. "Sorry if it was weird that I said Dan was cute. He seems really nice," she said. "It must be fun having an older brother instead of a younger one. Christopher is always getting into my stuff and bugging me!"

"Well, Dan is pretty nice," I admitted. "But wait until you hear the loud music he plays. That's really annoying."

Ava sat up. "So you must like living here, right?"

I shrugged. "It's okay. But I miss not seeing my dad every day. And you and everyone else."

"But you still get to see us," Ava said. "It's kind of like you have the best of both worlds."

"Maybe," I said, a little unsure. "Sometimes I think about what it would be like if things had never changed with my parents. Most of the time I think I would like that. But I'd miss some of this new stuff, like some of my new friends."

"I guess I would be sad if I couldn't see my dad every day," Ava said thoughtfully.

That's what I love about Ava. She gets me, you know?

"So listen to this," I said. "I am failing Spanish class!"

Ava looked surprised, and then she said the same thing everyone else always said: "But don't you speak Spanish?"

"*Sí,*" I replied, and then I explained the situation like I had to Katie and my cupcake friends. Ava nodded.

"It's the same with me," she said. "My dad's a

doctor, and I almost failed science! He was mad at first, but then when he was helping me with my homework, he saw how hard it was, so I had a tutor. It really helped."

I imagined Eddie and Mum sitting in Señora Delgado's class and smiled. "I wonder if Mum and Eddie could even do my homework. It's hard!"

"Just ask for help," Ava said. "They'll understand. I'm sure they'd rather help you than have you fail the class."

"I will," I told her, but I wasn't sure if I meant it. After all, things had been pretty crazy the last few months, with the move and the wedding and everything. Maybe I just needed to catch up, I told myself.

Suddenly a loud screeching came through the bedroom wall, followed by the *thump, thump, thump* of a bass line.

Ava covered her ears. "Oh my gosh! What *is* that?" she yelled over the music.

I grinned. "I told you!" I shouted back.

"DAN! Turn it DOWN!" I yelled, and banged on the wall. "Not so cute now, is he?" I said, and then we both started laughing.

CHAPTER 6

A Different Kind of Cupcake Meeting

Spending Saturday with Ava was awesome. We went to the shops, and after that Mum made spicy chili for dinner. Then we all watched a film together (well, except for Dan, who was out with his friends). And Ava and I stayed up *way* late talking and talking. I love my cupcake friends, but it's also great to have a friend who knows your history. Someone you don't see all the time, but every time you reconnect, you can pick up right where you left off. Every time I see Ava it's like we just hung out the day before.

In the morning we helped Mum make chocolate chip pancakes, and then we got the kitchen ready for the Cupcake Club meeting. Eddie was making a turkey-and-swiss sandwich on a superlong loaf of bread while I got out the baking stuff.

"I ordered the bread specially from the bakery," he told us. "This is a lunch meeting, right? You can't have a lunch meeting without lunch!"

I hadn't even thought about that. Eddie's pretty good that way. I think he likes to take care of people.

To tell the truth, I was a little bit nervous about the meeting. Besides baking the cinnamon-frosted cupcakes, we were also going to talk about the cupcakes we were making for Ava's birthday party in a few weeks. I was invited to the party, but my cupcake friends weren't.

Of course, we bake stuff all the time for events we're not invited to, like that baby shower for our science teacher's sister. So maybe that wasn't such a big deal.

I was also worried that Ava wouldn't get along with my Maple Grove friends. But then I realised that everyone is really nice, so that shouldn't be a problem. At least, I hoped it wouldn't be!

Then the bell rang, and Katie, Alexis and Emma all arrived at once. It took a few minutes for everyone to take off their coats, hats, gloves and scarves, but soon we were all around the kitchen table and Eddie was cutting up his giant sandwich for us.

"I like your shirts," Emma said to Ava. She was wearing the striped shirt with the butterfly shirt that she had borrowed from me.

"Thanks! They're Mia's," she replied. "The butterfly one has always been my favourite."

I noticed that Katie suddenly got kind of a weird look on her face. Was she jealous? No, probably not. *Katie's just insecure,* I thought. Her old best friend, Callie, dumped her, so she's always afraid someone else is going to do the same thing.

Then Ava started to talk really fast about stuff, like she does when she's excited or nervous.

"You guys live in such a nice town," she said. "I'm kind of jealous. I sort of wish I had an older brother like Dan too."

Emma rolled her eyes. "You're lucky. They can be *so* annoying."

"More annoying than a little brother?" Ava asked. "'Cause I already have one of those."

Emma nodded. "Worse. At least little brothers do cute things sometimes."

"I tried to tell you, Ava," I said.

"At least none of you have an older sister,"

Alexis chimed in. "She spends hours and hours in the bathroom every day."

"Dan showers longer than any of us," I whispered. "And then he sprays on that aftershave for guys that they advertise on TV. Gross!"

I looked at Katie, expecting her to make a joke like she always does, but she was kind of quiet. In fact, she stayed quiet for the rest of the meeting. I decided I'd have to ask her later if everything was okay.

Then Alexis took out her notebook and we got down to business.

"So, Ava, I can show you our most popular cupcake styles," she said.

Ava took her phone from her jeans pocket. "Actually, I have a list of ideas I've been working on," she said. "Mia says you guys can do anything, right?"

Alexis looked flustered – she's used to being the one in charge, and Ava was kind of taking over.

"Well, sure, but sometimes it helps if—"

"Let's hear your idea, Ava!" Emma said, smoothing things over.

"I have a few," Ava replied. "But winter is totally my favourite season, and it almost always snows on my birthday, so I was hoping you could do a snowy cupcake."

Alexis started flipping through her notebook. "Snowy. Hmm, I'm not sure exactly how we'd do that."

All of us were quiet for a minute. A snowy cupcake? That was tough. Then Katie came through, as usual.

"Remember Emma's cupcake from yesterday?" she blurted out. "What if we do coconut flakes on top of vanilla icing? Mia said the coconut looked just like snow."

I nodded. "That could work."

I jumped out of my seat and ran to the kitchen cabinet where I keep all my cupcake supplies. Eddie had cleared out a shelf just for me.

I came back with a big jar of glittery sugar sprinkles.

"How about white icing, coconut flakes and then some edible glitter, like this?" I suggested. "We could do a silver wrapper."

"That sounds nice," Ava said. "But do I get to see it first?"

"We'll take a photo and send it to you for approval," Alexis said. "But first you need to tell us what flavour of cake you want."

44

"Would chocolate be okay?" Ava asked. "The brown cake won't show through the vanilla frosting, will it?"

"No way," I said. "Especially if Katie's doing the frosting. She's the best."

"You guys are all just as good," Katie said, smiling a little for the first time.

"We'll do a test run at our next meeting, after we get the ingredients," Alexis said. "Today we've got to do a test batch of Mia's spicy cupcakes."

"I've got the red food colouring and the cinnamon and the Red Hots," I said.

Katie held up the canvas shopping bag she had brought with her. "I was talking to my mum about them, and she thought some other flavours might go nice with the cinnamon frosting instead of the red velvet. Like dark chocolate, maybe, or apple."

"Wow, they both sound good," Ava said.

"I thought we could try a batch of each," Katie suggested. "I brought the dark chocolate, and some applesauce and some extra spices, like ginger and cloves." Everyone agreed to try the two different kinds, and we quickly got to work measuring out the flour and other ingredients for the cake mix.

"Don't you use a recipe?" Ava asked.

"Sometimes," I said. "But mostly we know how to make a basic cake mix and then add extra flavours to it."

"Ooh, extra spices! *Muy caliente*, right, Mia?" Emma said, and everybody laughed. But that got me thinking about my Spanish class again. How was I ever going to tell my mum and dad and Eddie that I was failing Spanish? Ava was right. They would make sure I got the extra help I needed. And the longer I avoided telling them, the worse it was going to be. But still, the thought of telling them made my stomach feel queasy. Even though I knew it was crazy, I kept hoping that if I avoided the problem, somehow it would magically disappear.

"Earth to Mia!" said Katie, waving something under my nose. She held up an index card. "Mum gave me her recipe for the dark chocolate ones. The measurements are always a little different when there's chocolate," she explained to Ava.

Chocolate. Now that should have caught my attention. But I couldn't get my mind off my Spanish class. This was awful. Baking cupcakes with the Cupcake Club was one of my favourite things to do in the entire world, and now I couldn't even enjoy that. I kept throwing ingredients into the batter and stirring, stirring, stirring, wishing I could make my problems disappear the way the spices were disappearing into the chocolate cake mix.

Wait — spices in the chocolate batter? I tasted a little bit. *Whoa.* Intense. And not in a good way.

"Um, sorry, guys," I said. "I think I mixed up the two cake mixes. I added the spices to the dark chocolate batter by accident." Alexis frowned at the waste of ingredients, but everyone else was really nice. We've all ruined or burned batches of cupcakes at one time or another, so everyone was pretty forgiving.

"Maybe you should work on something else right now," Alexis suggested.

I agreed, and so I said, "Ava and I will do the icing." Then we made a double batch of vanilla icing dyed red and spiced with cinnamon.

About forty-five minutes later we were staring at two plates of cupcakes with red frosting and dotted with spicy sweets. They looked great, and both looked the same — although inside, they were both really different.

"Tasting time!" Alexis announced, and we cut

some of the cupcakes in half so we each ate half of one. Everyone got quiet for a few minutes while we ate. Cupcake tasting *is* fun, but it's also serious business.

"They are both so good," Emma said, wiping her mouth with a napkin. "But I think I like the dark chocolate ones best."

"Me too," I agreed.

Alexis shook her head. "I like the spices in the apple cupcakes."

"I vote for apple too," Katie said.

Alexis frowned. "It's a tie."

"Ava can break the tie," I said. "What do you think, Ava?"

"You know me. I love chocolate!" she replied.

I turned to my friends. "What do you think? Should we do the dark chocolate?"

Katie and Alexis looked at each other and shrugged.

"Fine," Alexis said. "Studies show that chocolate is one of the most popular cupcake flavours, anyway. Maybe we'll get some new customers from it."

"And they're Valentine's Day cupcakes," Emma said. "And you know how everybody goes gaga over chocolate on Valentine's Day."

Katie put her arms around the plate of apple

cupcakes. "Then I guess I'll be taking these home," she joked, and we all laughed.

It felt really good to have all my friends together in one place. But I knew it wouldn't last. In a little while, Ava would have to go back to the city. My cupcake friends would be in Maple Grove. And I would still be stuck with Spanish wherever I went.

CHAPTER 7

Tiny Plates and Tiny Lies

After our meeting was over and the kitchen was clean, Ava and I had to hurry and pack up her things. We had a half hour to get to the train station.

Even though Ava was leaving, there was one good thing about that day. You see, I was supposed to see my dad this weekend, but he had to go on a business trip. He was coming back Sunday afternoon, and Mum had to go to the city to style a client for a party, so she and I were going to take the train in with Ava. Mum would go to work, Ava would go home, and I'd get to have a special dinner with my dad.

It sounds complicated, right? Welcome to my life!

Eddie drove us to the train station and dropped us off. He gave Mum a big hug and a kiss. I looked at Ava and winced.

"He's acting like she's going away for a year or something," I said. "We'll be back in a few hours."

Ava laughed. "I don't know. I think it's kind of sweet."

I rolled my eyes. "Seriously?"

Then the train pulled up, and Mum and Ava and I climbed on. It wasn't as crowded as it usually is when I leave on Friday, so we all found a seat near one another. I don't really love the train, though. The seats are an ugly colour, and it always smells like stale bread in there. But it's fast and it gets me to my dad, so I don't mind so much.

Mum shopped for accessories on her tablet on the way to Manhattan, and Ava and I talked about her upcoming birthday party. The snowy cupcakes had inspired her.

"I could get silver and white decorations," she was saying. "And sprinkle silver glitter on the cake table, maybe."

I whipped out my sketchbook. "We could put the cupcakes at different heights, like this," I said, quickly drawing my vision for her.

"I love it!" Ava exclaimed.

"And of course you'll need the perfect dress," I said.

I flipped the page and started sketching Ava in a snowy dress – a sleeveless top attached to a flowing, white knee-length skirt.

"The top could be silver," I said, pointing. "But I'm not sure. It kind of looks like an ice skater's outfit."

"No, it's awesome," Ava said sincerely. "You are such a good designer, Mia! You're going to be famous someday."

I blushed a little bit, and Mum leaned over to see my sketch. She smiled. Being a famous fashion designer would be so cool. But I know that takes a lot of hard work, and a lot of luck, too.

Finally the train pulled into Penn Station. It's always crazy when everyone gets off the train, with people running in every direction, but Dad always waits in the same spot for me, by this big pillar by the ticket counter.

When the doors opened up and we walked to the concourse level, I saw him standing there. Dad always looks like a film star to me. He had on a warm black coat that wasn't puffy at all, and shiny black shoes and an olive green scarf around his neck. Dad wears glasses with black rims, but on him they don't look old-fashioned, they look smart.

I ran up and hugged him.

"Hello, *mija*!" he said. "It's good to see you."

Ava and my mum walked up behind me.

"Hello, Alex," my mum said. Her voice sounded friendly, but a little cold at the same time.

"Hi, Sara," dad replied, and he just sounded uncomfortable.

Ava looked around. "Where's my mum?" she asked.

"She texted me and said she's a little bit late," Mum answered. "But we'll all wait with you until she gets here."

And so we waited, and it was totally awkward. Mum and Dad were talking to me instead of each other.

"Mia, how are you doing in school?"

"Mia, is it colder in New Jersey?"

"Mia, tell your father about your Valentine's Day cupcakes."

I realised that this was probably the longest time my parents had spent in the same place since their divorce. No wonder it was awkward.

Finally, Mrs Monroe came rushing up. "I'm so sorry! The subways are so slow on Sunday."

"That's all right," Mum told her. "Thank you for letting Ava stay with us. She's a pleasure to have around."

"And so is Mia," Mrs Monroe said. She smiled at me. "We'll see you at the party soon. I can't wait to try your cupcakes!"

Ava gave me a quick hug good-bye. "I'll text you later," I said.

Then Mum kissed me. "I'll meet you back here at seven fifteen, okay?"

"I'll make sure she's on time," my dad promised.

"Thanks," Mum said, and managed a smile. She then rushed off, and it was just me and my dad.

"Sushi?" I asked. That's usually our tradition.

"Well, since this is a special visit, I thought we should mix it up a little bit," Dad said. "Try someplace new."

"Where are we going?" I asked him.

Dad smiled. "I want to surprise you."

So we quickly found a taxi outside and travelled downtown for a while. Then the taxi stopped in front of a restaurant with a red awning. Painted on the window were the words SABOR TAPAS BAR.

"We're going to a bar?" I asked. "Isn't that kind of inappropriate?"

"It's not that kind of bar," Dad said, paying the taxi driver. "You'll see."

We walked inside, and the place looked warm and cozy. Dark wood panels covered the walls, and the booths were made of wood too, with red cushions. The server showed us to one of the booths, and then Dad handed me a menu.

"In a tapas bar, they serve small plates of food," Dad explained. "And then you share. That way you get to try a little bit of a lot of different things."

The server, a woman with dark hair almost exactly like mine, took our drink orders, and then we looked at the menu. Everything on it looked delicious. I was starting to like this idea.

"This is awesome," I said. "But there's so much to choose from! I can't decide."

"I'll order for us, then," he said.

The server brought our drinks, and then Dad ordered a bunch of tapas from the menu: shrimp with garlic and chilies, a potato omelet, sautéed spinach and a bowl of Spanish olives.

"Anything else, *mija*?" he asked.

I looked at the menu, and one thing caught my eye.

"*Croquetas con pollo y plátanos, por favor,*" I

ordered. (That means "Croquettes with chicken and plantains, please." I wasn't sure what a croquette was, but I love plantains. They're kind of like bananas, but not sweet.)

"Bien. Creo que les gustará," the server replied in Spanish. That means, "Good. I think you'll like them."

"Creo que lo haré," I replied, which means, "I think that I will."

The server left the table, and when I looked at Dad, he was beaming with pride.

"Such good Spanish, *mija*," he said. "Your Spanish teacher must love you."

I smiled, but I didn't say a word. I know what you're thinking. This was the perfect time for me to talk to my dad about my problems in Advanced Spanish. I know Ava told me I should ask for help, but I just couldn't bear to disappoint Dad. Not now, anyway. I just wanted to have a nice dinner with him.

And it *was* nice. It turned out that a croquette is a little fried ball-shaped thing, and it was superdelicious. All the stuff Dad ordered tasted good too.

But it went way too fast, and soon it was time to get back to the train. Dad walked me to the platform, and Mum was already waiting there.

"Get home safe," Dad said, giving me a hug.

"I'll text you when I get home," I promised.

Mum got a funny look on her face. After Dad left, I found out why.

"You always complain when I ask you to text *me*," Mum said.

Yikes. She had a point. I had to think about that for a little bit.

"You have me most of the time, plus Eddie and Dan, but Dad is all alone," I explained. "I feel bad for Dad sometimes."

Mum sighed. "It's hard," she admitted, "but please don't worry about your dad, Mia. I know he misses you a lot, but he's still your dad, no matter where we live. And we're all a lot happier this way."

Happier? I had to think about that one.

As the train sped towards Maple Grove, I stared out the window into the dark sky. Mum and Dad fought a *lot* before they got divorced. They tried to do it at night in their room, when they thought I was asleep, but I always heard them. So I guess they weren't too happy then.

But when they got divorced, things still weren't good. Mum moved out and I stayed with

Dad, but it felt weird and I missed her. And Mum and Dad still argued every time they saw each other. Then I moved into Mum's new flat, but that was extra weird because it was a whole new place.

So was it still weird? I had to think about that. Living in Maple Grove was starting to feel like home. I had good friends. And Eddie and Dan were nice, and Eddie sure tried to make us feel like a "normal" family as much as possible. But happi-*er*? As in, more happy than before, when we were all together?

Like I said, I'd have to think about that.

CHAPTER 8

Can I Start the Week Over Again?

While I was still on the train, I called Katie. I wanted to reach her before it got too late.

"Hey," I said.

"Hey," Katie replied. "Are you home?"

"I'm on the train," I told her. "Is everything okay? You seemed a little quiet at the meeting today."

"Everything's fine," Katie said, but I could tell by the sound of her voice that she was lying.

"Good," I said. I wasn't going to press her about it. "So anyway, we're still going to see *The Emerald Forest* next weekend, right?"

"Of course!" Katie answered, and her voice sounded like the old Katie again. The Emerald Forest is a fantasy book series that we both love, and they finally made a film out of it!

"Awesome," I said. "I can't wait to see what kind of costumes they're going to do for the emerald fairies. In the books, the description is totally beautiful."

"I can't wait either," Katie agreed. "We're going on Saturday, right?"

"Mum said she'll take us," I promised.

We said good night, and I hung up the phone. When I got home, I was totally exhausted. I fell asleep dreaming of the Emerald Forest. . .

If only the rest of the week was as peaceful as that forest. But it was anything but. The next day was Monday, my least favourite day of the week.

I was so tired in the morning that I left my gym uniform home by mistake, and I had to sit out of gym. And Señora Delgado gave us pages and pages of notes for our Spanish test the next day – on verbs.

You have to believe me when I tell you that I studied like crazy. I went straight home after school and studied. I ate dinner and then went right back upstairs and studied. I didn't even sketch! (Okay, I did doodle a pair of boots in the margin of my notes, but I didn't open up my sketchbook, I swear.) When I went to sleep that night, I dreamed of verbs instead of emerald fairies.

I even studied at lunch on Tuesday before the test. I was feeling pretty good – until Señora handed me my test paper. The questions looked like Egyptian hieroglyphics to me.

So I took the test, and I did my best. But as I handed it in, I knew I hadn't done well.

That night Mum asked me about it as we were cleaning up from dinner.

"So how did you do on your Spanish test?" she asked. "You really studied hard for that one."

"I think I did okay," I lied. I thought about spilling everything out, right then and there. *Mum, I think I'm failing Spanish. I know I should have told you sooner. The advanced class is so difficult. I'm still having trouble no matter how hard I try.* I opened my mouth to tell her, but I just couldn't bring myself to say the words. I don't know why it was so hard. Usually I could always talk to Mum about anything.

It was then that I realised that Mum really was a lot happier. She smiled a lot, and she seemed more relaxed than ever, even though she was busy. And she really did seem to love Eddie. Then I wondered if my dad was as happy as Mum. Was I?

Mum smiled at me and kissed the top of my head. "I'm so proud of you, Mia," she said.

Ugh. I felt bad about lying, and then something happened that made me feel ten times worse.

"I have a surprise for you," she said. "Come upstairs with me."

I followed Mum to her room. "So you know that Annie Chang has a line out for teens, right?"

I nodded. Annie Chang is a popular fashion designer, and I absolutely love her clothes. I was psyched when I read that she was putting out a teen line. But I know they are kind of expensive, too, so I wasn't holding out much hope that I'd convince Mum to buy me anything.

Mum unzipped a garment bag hanging from her closet. "I met Annie at an event the other day, and I told her all about you," she said. "So today she sent this just for you."

I gasped. Inside the bag was a totally cool mod-looking jumper dress with grey and black stripes.

"That's from her latest winter line!" I shrieked. "Oh, Mum, it's perfect!"

"Wear it with some black tights – or even a jewel-toned colour, for that matter – and black boots, and you've got a killer outfit," Mum said.

I slipped the dress off the hanger and ran to my room. "I'm going to try it on!"

I tried the dress with some solid red tights, and it looked awesome. I ran into my mum's room and gave her a big hug.

"Thank you, thank you!" I said.

"You deserve it, with all the hard work you've been doing," Mum said, and I felt a huge pang of guilt.

You should tell her now, a little voice inside me said. But just like Dad and dinner, I didn't want to ruin the moment.

I loved the dress so much that I wanted to sleep in it, but I didn't want to ruin it. So I wore it to school the very next day. At lunchtime, I was walking past the PGC table when Callie called out to me.

"Mia? Is that an Annie Chang?" she asked.

I walked over to her. "Yes, she gave it to my mum to give to me," I said.

"It's really cool," said Maggie, another one of the popular girls. Maggie's actually pretty nice, but she does everything Sydney tells her to do.

Sydney examined my entire outfit from head to toe. I could tell she was trying to find something wrong with it, but she couldn't. So she just made one of her mean comments instead. "It's nice of your mum's friends to give you their castoffs," Sydney said, tossing her perfect blonde hair. I knew she was insulting me, but I didn't care.

I smiled sweetly at Sydney. "Yeah, well, Mum says that Annie *is* really nice," I said. "And it's actually not a castoff. It's a sample. Like the kind they give models to wear. See you."

Then I walked away.

My Cupcake Club friends liked my dress too, even though they didn't know who Annie Chang was. Then it was time for Spanish class. Oh boy.

Señora Delgado handed out our tests as soon as we sat down. I already knew how I did, but I was still shocked when I saw the big red F on my paper. I've never gotten an F in anything before.

"Class, please turn to page fifty-seven in your workbooks and start that page," she said in Spanish, as usual. "Ms Vélaz-Cruz, please come to my desk."

Uh-oh. This wasn't going to be fun. I walked up to her desk as slowly as I could. What was she going to do? Was she going to yell at me in front of everybody?

Señora Delgado is petite, with short black hair, and she wears big eyeglasses. She looks like a very wise owl. And I know from science class that owls are predators. They eat cute little chipmunks and mice.

"Mia, I think you might need some extra help in this class," she said softly, in English. She wasn't mean or angry at all. It seemed like she really wanted to help me. She started to write on a piece of paper. "I know some excellent tutors. Please give this to your parents and tell them to call me if they have any questions."

"Thank you, Señora," I said quietly, and then I walked back to my seat. I couldn't keep my secret any longer now. I'd have to give my parents the note. But I didn't have to give it to them right away.

I'll give it to them, I told myself, *when the time is right! Because they're all too happy now for me to spoil it.*

CHAPTER 9

Sydney Needs My Help. Really?

Okay, so I technically couldn't give my parents the note that night because my dad was in Manhattan and my mum was working late. It was just me and Eddie and Dan, and Eddie is technically my *step*parent, not my parent. So I left the note in my Spanish book.

We had a Cupcake Club meeting at Katie's house the next day after school. Katie's mum was there. Mrs Brown has curly brown hair and Katie's smile, and she's really nice. She's the one who taught Katie how to make cupcakes.

"Come on in, girls, I've got it all set up for you," Mrs Brown said as we went into the kitchen. Katie's kitchen is small, but it's got everything you need to make cupcakes in it. Her mum has every kitchen gadget you've ever heard of – and some you haven't heard of.

We quickly got to work making a test batch of Ava's snowy cupcakes. Katie and I made the chocolate cake mix, and Emma and Alexis worked on the extra frosting.

"I want to get it extra fluffy," Emma said as they put the ingredients in the mixer bowl. "So it looks like snow."

"Great idea," I said. I opened up my bag. "Good news! My mum found the silver cupcake liners for us."

"She's so nice," Katie said, smiling at me, and I figured that whatever was bothering her wasn't anymore. Maybe she was just uncomfortable around people she didn't know, and that's why she was quiet when Ava was visiting.

As we baked the cupcakes we talked about school and stuff, and then Katie asked me, "So how did you do on that Spanish test?"

I frowned. "I can't bear to say it." Instead, I used the wooden spoon in my hand to draw an *F* in the bowl of batter.

"You failed? No way!" Katie cried. "But you studied so hard."

"I know," I said. "Señora says I need a tutor."

"Will your parents get you one?" Emma asked.

I bit my lower lip. "Well, they kind of don't know yet. I'm waiting for the right moment to tell them."

"That must be so hard," Katie said sympathetically.

"You should tell them soon," said Alexis, always the practical one. "They're going to find out eventually. And the sooner you get some help in Spanish, the better. You've put this off long enough. I thought maybe if you studied a little harder, you'd be okay, but things are obviously getting worse instead of better."

"Just talk to your mum, Mia," Katie said. "I'm sure once you tell her everything, it will be all right."

"I know, I know!" I said crossly. "Can we please talk about cupcakes instead of school?"

Nobody said anything for a while after that, and I felt kind of bad for losing it. But soon we were back in our groove again, and I was decorating our first test cupcake.

"It's perfect!" Alexis said, and I had to admit it looked pretty good. The silver liner was really pretty, the icing was nice and fluffy and the sparkles looked good on top of the coconut.

"Let me take a picture and I'll send it to Ava," I said.

A minute later Ava texted me back.

It's pretty, but the coconut looks too big or something. Not like snowflakes.

Alexis rolled her eyes. "Great. Another picky client."

"Hey, she's my friend," I reminded her. "Besides, she kind of has a point."

The coconut flakes from the package did look a little big. Luckily for us, Mrs Brown walked in just then.

"That's beautiful!" she said.

"Except Ava doesn't like it," Katie said, and then explained about the coconut.

Katie's mum looked thoughtful. "I think I have just the thing," she said finally.

She opened up the small pantry closet by the back door and came back with a weird-looking device.

"It's a veggie chopper," she said. "Normally you could use it to chop onions into small pieces. But I bet it will work on the coconut."

She put a pile of coconut on a cutting board,

put the chopper on top of it, and then pressed down a few times. When she picked up the chopper, the coconut underneath was very finely shredded.

"That looks a lot more like snow," Katie remarked. "Let's try another one."

So Katie iced another cupcake, and I sprinkled the coconut flakes and glittery sugar on top.

"Much better," agreed Mrs Brown. "I'm sure your friend will like it."

"Let's see," I said. I sent another photo to Ava. This time she was happy. Here was her reply:

♥♥♥♥♥♥♥

"She loves it!" I reported, and we all cheered.

"I think I've got all the details down so we can re-create this for the party," Alexis said. "Otherwise, we're meeting at my house on Saturday morning to do the Valentine's cupcakes, right?"

"Right," Emma said.

"My mum said she'd help us drop them off at the bookstore," I told them.

Alexis shut her notebook. "Just one more thing," she said. She gave each of us a sheet of paper. "Let me know what you think, and then I'll get the ad up on the PTA website next week."

We all read Alexis's ad:

Need a sweet treat for your next party or event? Let us do the baking for you! Click here to contact the Cupcake Club. We can do any flavour or amount you want. And we're having a baker's dozen special for all new customers! Buy a dozen cupcakes and get one free!

"I like the 'sweet treat' part," Katie said.

"It's really good, Alexis," Emma said.

I nodded. "The baker's dozen was a great idea, Katie," I said. "I'll bet we'll get lots of new business from this."

When the meeting was over, Eddie picked me up and brought me home. Mum was home, but she was working in her office. And at dinner she seemed really distracted. So I decided it wouldn't be fair to give her the note while she was so busy.

The next day was Friday, and I was glad it was the last day of the week. No tests, and we had our leftover snowy cupcakes for Cupcake Friday.

But then something really unexpected happened at lunch. Here's how it went down. While I was eating lunch, Sydney Whitman actually came up to our lunch table.

"Mia, can I talk to you a minute?" she asked. "I need a favour."

"Sure," I said. I turned to my friends and raised my eyebrows, giving that *I don't know what she wants* look. Then I followed her over to the wall.

"Thanks," she said. "I got this text from Jackson Montano, and it's in Spanish. Usually I'd ask Callie, but she's home because she's sick today."

What could I say? Should I launch into my entire "I can speak Spanish really well, but I have problems reading and writing it" explanation? Meanwhile, Queen Sydney stood in front of me with her arms crossed, waiting for me to say something.

"Uh, sure," I said, a little nervously. I hoped it wasn't too complicated.

Sydney handed me her phone, and I checked the message.

Te quiero.

Now, if you read Spanish you probably know that this means, "I love you," which is what my parents say to me, and my *abuela* says all the time. But when I saw "*quiero*" I got it mixed up with the word "*queso*," which means "cheese."

Yes, that's right. That's what I thought. And here's what I told Sydney.

"He says you're cheesy," I said.

Honestly, I didn't think that was strange. Jackson is on the football team, and he says mean things to kids all the time. Sydney and Jackson actually would make a perfect couple. Jackson thinks he's supercool just because he's a football player, and Sydney thinks she's supercool because . . . well, because she's Sydney.

Sydney's face turned bright red. "Cheesy? Really? I'll show him!"

Then she stomped away. She went back to her table, and I could see her talking with Maggie. While Sydney talked, she looked shocked and kept glancing down at her phone and looked like she was getting angrier by the minute.

I went back to the table.

"What did she want?" Alexis asked.

I shrugged. "She wanted me to translate some text message for her from Jackson Montano. He

73

told her he thinks she's cheesy."

"Cheesy? That's a weird thing to say," Emma said.

"Hmm. Well, at least that's one less boy drooling over Sydney," Katie said. "So yay for that."

"It figures he's texting her," Alexis said. "Those two think alike."

And then I forgot all about it – for a little while, anyway. In a split second, I had made a terrible mistake – one that would haunt me forever. (I know that sounds totally dramatic, but it's true!)

CHAPTER 10

Katie Is Still Acting Weird

That night at dinner Mum made an announcement.

"I just got the e-mails about the parent-teacher conferences next week," she said. "I can't wait to meet all your teachers!"

I almost choked on my pork chop, and started coughing.

"Mia, are you okay?" Mum asked.

I nodded and took a sip of water.

"Do not believe anything Mrs Caldwell tells you," Dan said. "She's always accusing me of messing around in class, but it's Joseph, not me."

Eddie raised an eyebrow. "Hmm, we'll see about that," he said. "Any other teachers we should look out for?"

Dan shrugged. "They're all pretty cool, I guess.

Mr Bender gives us tons of homework, but I always do it all."

"What about you, Mia?" Eddie asked.

I shrugged too. "They're all cool." Normally, I would have told them about how much fun Ms Biddle's science class is and how strict Mrs Moore is in math class, but I didn't feel like talking. I couldn't keep my secret about Spanish class much longer. I decided I'd have to tell Mum after dinner.

But then Eddie said something that really made me mad.

"Mia, I'm looking forward to meeting your teachers too," he said.

I almost choked again. Why was Eddie going to my parent-teacher conference? Dad is the one who should be going!

I was too angry to say anything. I kept quiet until the end of dinner. Then after, when Mum and I were cleaning up, I confronted her.

"Why is Eddie going instead of Dad?" I asked her. "Dad's still my parent, right? Shouldn't he be going?"

Mum looked really startled. "Well . . ." she said, like she was trying to figure out an answer. "I didn't think of it. It might be hard for Dad to get here from the city during the week. I'll ask him. But is there a reason you don't want Eddie to go?"

"Because he's not my dad!" I blurted out.

Mum sat down on the nearest chair. She thought for a minute.

"You're right about that," she said finally. "But he's still your parent. He cares about you very much. And he takes an active role with you. He helps you with your homework and projects. So it's important for him to meet your teachers and know what's going on in your school."

I nodded grudgingly, feeling a little guilty. After all, Eddie did drive me all over the place, and he made me lunch and dinner and snacks. But I was still mad. "Fine. But Dad does those things too. He should be there."

"I promise I'll talk to him," Mum said. "And if he can't go, I'll make sure he gets all the information, okay?"

"Okay," I mumbled. Then I went up to my room. I decided to do some sketching. Sketching always relaxes me and makes me feel better when I'm in a bad mood.

I started to sketch some Valentine's Day outfits. First I drew a really girlie pink dress with a short, full skirt that I knew Emma would love. Then I drew a denim skirt paired with a loose jumper, with a big bold red heart embroidered on the front. It looked very "casual cool." Out of the blue I wondered how I would write "casual cool" in Spanish. I drew a complete blank. I couldn't stop thinking about it, and I found myself getting more and more upset. *Great,* I thought. *Now even my sketch time is ruined by Spanish.* Meanwhile, I had forgotten all about giving Mum the note from Señora Delgado.

The next morning I woke up early, and Mum drove me to Alexis's house. She has the neatest, cleanest kitchen of all of us. We had to get the cupcakes to the bookstore by one o'clock, so we got to work right away.

Katie and I worked on the cinnamon-frosted cupcakes, and Emma and Alexis worked on the pretty pink cupcakes. Emma blasted some music, and we didn't talk much while we worked. Katie calls it "being in the baking zone."

When we were done, we had four dozen perfect, beautiful cupcakes packed neatly into boxes. I had designed labels for us on the computer that said THE CUPCAKE CLUB, and there was a picture of a cupcake on each one. I carefully stuck a label on each box, and we stepped back to admire our hard work.

"Perfect!" Alexis said with satisfaction.

I looked at the clock, and it was ten minutes to noon. "Mum will be here soon. She's going to take Katie and me to lunch, and then we're going to drop off the cupcakes and then see the film. Are you sure you guys don't want to go?"

"I've got three dog walking clients today," Emma said. "Otherwise I would."

"And we're all going to my grandmother's house today," Alexis said. "But text me when the movie's done! I'm dying to see it."

"Even though I already know how it ends, I still can't wait," Katie said. She looked really excited.

Then Alexis handed me an envelope. "I printed out some business cards on my computer using your label design," she said. "See if you can leave them out on the cupcake table. That way if anyone likes the cupcakes and wants to order some, they know how to reach us."

My mum then came in, and she helped us carry the boxes to the car. We have an organiser in our trunk now, so the boxes don't slide around. The bookstore, Harriet's Hollow, is in downtown Maple Grove. There are a bunch of other stores on Main Street besides Harriet's. There's also a little café where they have the most awesome tuna melts. That's where we went for lunch.

"Mmm, melty!" Katie said when her sandwich came, and we all laughed.

Then it was time to deliver the cupcakes to Harriet's. The owner of the store is named Harriet. She's tall and has long brown hair that she always piles on her head, and she has a very global sense of fashion. Today she was wearing a really flowy purple-and-orange dress that looked like it was made from Indian saris, and she had lots of silver bracelets jangling on her wrists.

"It's the cupcake girls!" she said when she saw us. "And right on time, too. Come here, let me show you the display."

We walked through the store to the place in the back that Harriet called the reading nook. It's filled with comfy couches and beanbag chairs, and Harriet doesn't mind if you sit there and read all day. Today she had decorated it with pink and red flowers on the end tables, and in the middle was a round table with a pink tablecloth on it.

"We'll set them up for you," Katie said, and we started by putting out four round, clear plastic trays that we got from a party store. They don't cost much, and the cupcakes look good on them. Then we carefully placed the cupcakes on them: two trays of my spicy dark chocolate with cinnamon frosting, and two trays of Emma's fluffy pink cupcakes.

"They look too good to eat!" Harriet exclaimed, but then she picked up a spicy one. "But of course I can't resist."

Katie and I held our breath while Harriet took a bite. We always get a little nervous when someone tries our cupcakes for the first time.

Harriet smiled. "Fantastic!" she said. "What's in this?"

Katie and I explained the flavours of the two cupcakes, and Harriet nodded in approval. She walked to the register and came back with an envelope for us.

"Thank you so much, girls," she said. "I'll be sure to recommend you to my friends."

Then I remembered Alexis's cards. "We have some business cards," I said. "Would it be okay if we put some out on the table?"

"Of course!" Harriet said. "My, you girls certainly are professional."

I made a mental note to tell Alexis that later. She would love that compliment!

Next Mum dropped us off at the cinema, which is in the shopping centre. Now that we're in middle school, our mums have decided that we can go to see films by ourselves, as long as we don't leave the cinema. (Eddie didn't like that idea much, but Mum convinced him.)

Soon Katie and I were sitting in our seats with drinks and a bucket of popcorn between us. They were showing some adverts or something on the screen, so I started to tell Katie about my problems with Mum and Eddie and Spanish.

"It's bad enough that everyone's going to find out that I'm failing, but I don't really get why Eddie needs to go," I said. "My dad should go, right?"

"I guess," Katie answered. She really didn't seem interested, but I kept talking.

"Plus, I have to check in with everyone all the time," I said. "It's like I have three police officers watching my every move or something. I feel like a prisoner sometimes. We're lucky Eddie's not sitting here right now."

"Shh," Katie said. "The previews are coming on."

I have to admit I was a little bit hurt about that. It's like Katie didn't care at all, which isn't like her. Usually she's a great person to talk to.

As the previews played, I tried to figure out what might be bugging her. I know Katie's parents are divorced too, so I figured she'd understand.

Then it hit me — Katie never talks about her dad, ever, and she doesn't visit him the way I do. I don't know why, but she just doesn't. Maybe her dad lives far away or something. I've never really asked her.

So maybe Katie can't understand my problems. Maybe she has some of her own — different ones.

I almost asked her about it but then the lights went dark, and we both got transported to the Emerald Forest.

CHAPTER II

Sydney's Revenge

Katie was like her old self again after the film, so I didn't bring up anything about her dad. I figured she'd talk to me when she was ready.

Nothing much interesting happened until Monday morning, during my first maths lesson. Mrs Moore was explaining a problem on the board when suddenly a note fell onto my desk.

I looked up, alarmed. Mrs Moore is superstrict, and it takes guts to throw a note in her class. I looked around and saw Bella looking at me.

Bella is in the PGC (Popular Girls Club) with Sydney and Maggie and Callie. She's pretty quiet, but everyone knows she loves vampires – after all, she changed her named from Brenda to Bella because of that series with the sparkly vampires.

She dresses in black a lot and wears pale makeup.

Bella nodded for me to open the note, and I opened it.

Jackson Montano is going bald!
Seriously, it's true!

I gave Bella a strange look. What was that about? But then I saw Mrs Moore turn away from the board, and I quickly stashed the note in my book.

As Mrs Moore kept explaining fractions, I suddenly realised what the note was about. Sydney had said that Jackson would be sorry about calling her cheesy, and she meant it.

I showed the note to my friends at lunch, but nobody was surprised.

"There are these texts going around saying that Jackson has foot fungus," Alexis reported.

"I heard it in the hallway," Katie said. "Sydney, Bella and Maggie were telling everyone who would listen."

"Poor Jackson," Emma said sympathetically.

"I don't feel sorry for him," Alexis said. "He always calls me 'copper top' and asks if my brains are rusting."

"And George says he's mean to the younger kids on the football team," Katie added. George is her friend from primary school, and Jackson is one year above us, so I guess he must pick on George.

"Still, nobody deserves the Sydney treatment," I said.

"Well, nobody actually believes this stuff, do they?" Katie asked. "Maggie told me that he has false teeth. I mean, come on."

"It doesn't matter if they believe it or not," Alexis pointed out. "It still looks bad for Jackson. Just imagine if Sydney were spreading those rumors about us."

I shuddered. "That would be awful. But I guess Jackson brought this on himself. He shouldn't have called her cheesy."

I still didn't know that I was the one who was causing Jackson so much trouble. But in the meantime, I still had plenty of other things to worry about – namely, my Spanish.

I had to tell the truth before the parent–teacher conference. It was the only thing to do. And that wasn't going to make anybody happy.

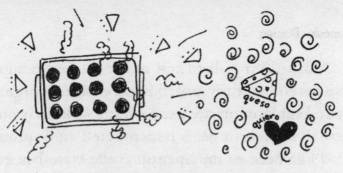

CHAPTER 12

A Really, Really Bad Day

𝒜s you can probably guess by now, I like to avoid bad situations. There didn't seem to be a time all week that I could talk to my mum. But that weekend I went to my dad's, and that's when it all came out.

It was after dinner on Friday, and I knew I had to bring up the note from Señora Delgado. But as you know, I love to put things off. So I decided to bake a batch of cupcakes first. My dad loves chocolate, so I made a quick, easy batch of chocolate cupcakes. Soon a delicious, chocolaty aroma was wafting through the entire flat.

"Something sure smells good, *mija*," Dad said with a smile as he walked past the kitchen.

"They'll be ready soon," I promised.

When Dad walked out of the kitchen, I took the note out of my notebook. For the millionth time, I replayed in my head what I would say and how I would say it. I remembered how proud Dad had been of my Spanish at the tapas bar. He was going to be so disappointed in me. I dreaded giving him this note, and I dreaded telling my mum, too.

As I sat staring forlornly at the note, my dad came running back into the kitchen.

"Mia! Don't you smell that?" he shouted. I looked up, confused, and was shocked to see black smoke coming out of the oven. The cupcakes were burning! My life really was in shambles. Now I couldn't even bake cupcakes anymore. Dad quickly turned off the oven and turned to look at me.

"*Mija*, is something wrong? You've never burned a batch of cupcakes before – especially when you were sitting two feet away from the oven. Is there anything you want to tell me or talk about?" I couldn't put it off any longer. Taking a deep breath, I took the note from Señora Delgado and handed it to him without saying anything.

Dad read it and raised his eyebrows. "Mia, what is this? You're failing Spanish? How is that possible?"

Tears filled my eyes. I couldn't help it.

"You guys put me in Advanced Spanish," I said. "It's really hard. I know I can speak it, but reading and writing it is different. My essays and homework are just too hard for me."

"They can't be that bad," Dad said. "Can you show me?"

I nodded and brought my backpack to the kitchen table, and Dad and I sat down.

"This is the worksheet she gave us for the weekend," I said, handing him the paper. It was another sheet of verbs.

Dad looked it over for a few minutes, and then he frowned. "You're right," he said. "I speak Spanish too, but this looks hard. Have you told Mum about this yet?"

I shook my head. "No," I admitted.

Dad sighed. "Well, I'll have to talk to her about this. We should talk to your teacher and get you one of these tutors she's suggesting."

"You can talk to her at the parent-teacher conference on Wednesday," I said, and Dad looked surprised.

"Wednesday? I don't think Mum mentioned that," he said.

I started to cry again. "Mum's going to be so mad when she finds out."

"*Mija*, we only get upset when you keep things from us. Having trouble in school is nothing to be ashamed of," Dad said, hugging me. "No matter what, *te quiero.*"

Te quiero. Dad had said those words to me a million times, and I knew what they meant: I love you. *Te quiero.*

Suddenly it hit me. "Dad, how do you spell *quiero*?" I yelled, breaking away from him.

"*Q-u-i-e-r-o,*" Dad answered. "That's one I know. Why?"

My stomach dropped down into my black velvet flats. I had made a terrible mistake.

"And how do you spell 'cheese' in Spanish?" I asked him.

"*Queso. Q-u-e-s-o,*" he replied.

"Oh no!" I wailed. "Oh no, no, no!"

I should have *known* that *quiero* meant "love," not "cheesy." Now Sydney thought Jackson had dissed her when actually he liked her. I felt awful! And now she was spreading all those awful rumours about him. So even if Jackson had liked Sydney to begin with, maybe I ruined it for her. I don't like Sydney, but I'd never purposely mess up anybody's budding romance.

"What's wrong, *mija*?" Dad asked.

"I made a terrible mistake." I groaned, and then I told him about Sydney and the note. Dad started to laugh and then stopped himself.

"Sorry. I know it's not funny to you," he said. "And I feel sorry for that boy. Sydney sounds like somebody you don't want to mess with."

"You don't even know," I said, shaking my head.

Dad put his hand over his mouth as he started to laugh again. "Oh, Mia. 'Cheese' instead of 'love'?" Then he saw I wasn't laughing. He put his arm around me again. "Come on, let's watch that film."

Soon we were settled in the living room with some microwave popcorn, and for a little while I forgot about all my problems while we watched a comedy about talking animals in a zoo. Then I got ready for bed.

Before I fell asleep, I heard Dad call Mum. He was talking in Spanish, but I heard most of it. His voice drifted in and out as he paced across the floor.

"You need to tell me these things, Sara! Just because I'm in Manhattan doesn't mean I don't want to be involved! You're the one who moved away, not me!"

For a second, it reminded me of a few years ago all over again, when Dad and Mum were fighting all the time. I put the pillow over my head, so I wouldn't hear.

See what happens when I tell the truth? It always ends up badly. I told you nobody would be happy.

CHAPTER 13

Just Like Old Times . . . Or Is It?

Saturday was a much better day. Mrs Monroe took me and Ava to see the Costume Collection at the Metropolitan Museum of Art. Ava and I took lots of pictures, and I spent about an hour sketching shoes from the 1920s. I liked the really cool buttons on them. Saturday night Dad and I went out for sushi, and everything felt like normal.

Then Sunday morning at eleven thirty, Dad said, "Mia, please pack your bag."

"But it's too early for the train," I told him.

"We're not going right to the train," he said. "Mum's meeting us for lunch at Johnny's Pizza."

At first I wasn't sure I'd heard right. Meeting Mum for lunch? Dad and Mum and I hadn't had lunch together since they got divorced.

I must be in big trouble, I thought. So I packed my bag and put on my coat, and then Dad and I headed out to Johnny's.

Johnny's has the best pizza in our neighbourhood, and maybe even in the whole city. They cook it in a brick oven with real wood, and the crust gets nice and crispy. Mum and Dad and I ate there a lot when we all lived together.

I shivered the whole walk there, but once we got inside it was warm and toasty. Mum was already sitting at a table, waiting for us. She had her hair pulled back, and she looked kind of tired.

Mum stood up when she saw us. "Hi, Mia," she said, giving me a hug. But she didn't hug Dad.

Dad draped his coat around the chair. "I'll go place our order," he said, and then he got in line.

Mum looked at me and shook her head. "Mia, your father told me about that note from your Spanish teacher. Why didn't you tell me?"

"I don't know," I said, looking down at the table. It was too hard to explain.

"You know can talk to me about these things, Mia," Mum said. "I just don't understand."

Dad sat down. "It should be ready in a few minutes," he said. "So, Mia, I guess you know why we're all here."

I nodded.

"It's like I said the other night," he said. "You can't keep secrets from us. Especially when it's about school and especially when you need help."

"That's right," Mum said, and she sounded angry. "Mia, your only job right now in life is to do well in school. Baking cupcakes, going to fashion shows, that's all good, but school is the most important."

"I know!" I said. "I really do. I'm doing well in my other classes. But you guys put me in Advanced Spanish without asking me. It's not my fault."

Dad and Mum looked at each other.

"I'm sorry about that," Dad said. "We didn't realise we were pushing you into something too hard for you. Sara, can they put her in a different class?"

"I'm not sure," Mum replied. "But I'll ask. I don't know if they can switch her schedule until the spring."

"In the meantime, we can get you a tutor," Dad said. He handed Mum the note. "Her teacher suggested a few."

"We might not need one," Mum said. "Eddie majored in Spanish in college. He's a translator at the company he works for."

I was surprised. "He is?" I asked.

"I thought you knew," Mum said. "What did you think he did?"

I shrugged. I knew Eddie was a lawyer, but I didn't know he also translated. "I don't know. I thought he just went to an office and . . . did stuff." Now I felt kind of silly not asking for help when I had an honest-to-goodness translator living right under the same roof as me.

"Then let's see if Eddie can help," Dad said. "But if not, we'll get you that tutor, okay?"

"Okay," I said.

"And no more secrets," Mum said sternly. "In fact, you can live without screens this week while you think about that. No phone, TV, music or computer. And if you keep any notes from teachers from us in the future, it will be *two* weeks."

I saw her look at Dad, and Dad gave a little nod.

I didn't even protest. With a sigh, I handed over my music player and earbuds, and my phone.

Luckily, Dad saw our order appear at the counter right then. "Food's ready! I'll be right back."

The rest of the lunch was a lot easier. We ate salads with vinegary dressing and these light green peppers that were sweet and hot at the same time. Then we had our usual – pizza with mushrooms and olives. (I know it sounds weird, but it's really good, trust me.)

For a minute, it almost seemed like old times, like nothing had changed. Except really, everything had. Before, Mum and Dad would have been talking and laughing the whole time. Now they couldn't even look at each other. Just like that other day, they both talked to me instead of each other.

And then, instead of all of us going back home, Mum and I got into a cab and headed to the train station. Back to Maple Grove. Back to our new life.

Things were never going to be the way they'd been before. I knew that. But knowing that didn't make it any easier. Was everyone really happier?

CHAPTER 14

A Cheesy Problem

When we got home, Mum and I met Eddie in the kitchen, and she told him the whole story.

"I think I can help you," Eddie said. "Let's take a look at your homework together after dinner, okay?"

I nodded, grateful that Eddie didn't give me a hard time about it all. After dinner that night, he and I sat at the kitchen table, and I showed him my worksheet.

"It's verbs I have trouble with," I told him. "There's, like, a million different ways to say and spell each one, and I can't keep them straight in my head."

"Let me see," Eddie said, taking the sheet. He looked it over and then smiled. "I used to have trouble with this too. But let me show you a trick I figured out."

So, I won't bore you with a whole Spanish lesson, but you need to know that by the time Eddie had finished helping me, I actually understood what was on the sheet. I answered every question, and Eddie didn't even have to help me with the last two. It was the first time I'd ever felt good about handing in my Spanish homework.

"Thanks, Eddie," I said when we were done.

Even though the tutoring went well, I was still feeling pretty down that night. That's because I knew that tomorrow I'd have to tell Sydney about the *quiero/queso* mistake.

I could keep the Spanish secret for so long because I was only hurting myself. But the *queso* secret was hurting Jackson, and it would be wrong if I didn't say anything.

But I was dreading it. I saw what Sydney did to Jackson when she was mad at him. She was going to destroy me, I just knew it.

So the next day, Monday, I knew what I had to do. As soon as I got off the bus, I walked up to Sydney. She and Maggie were hanging out by the tree in the front school yard, texting.

"Sydney, can I talk to you?" I asked.

"Busy," she said, not even looking up from her phone. "Later, okay?"

I tried again in the hallway, when I ran up to Sydney at her locker. She was talking to Eddie Rossi, but I interrupted her.

"Can I please talk to you?" I asked.

Sydney rolled her eyes. "Excuse me? Talking!"

My face turned red, and I walked away. For a second, I thought I might give up and let her keep torturing Jackson. But I just couldn't do that.

So at lunchtime, I marched up to the PGC table.

"Sydney, I need to tell you something really important," I said.

Sydney turned to Maggie and rolled her eyes. Then she looked at me.

"What's the emergency?" she asked.

"It's about that text message Jackson sent you," I said. "I made a mistake. He didn't say you're cheesy. He said he loves you."

Sydney looked absolutely shocked. "He *what*?" she shrieked.

"*Te quiero* means 'I love you,'" I explained. "I got it mixed up with the word *queso*, which means 'cheese.' I'm sorry."

Sydney stood up. "Are you kidding me?" she

asked, her voice rising. "Are you trying to ruin my life or something? Are you jealous? I bet you did that on purpose."

I shook my head. "No. I wouldn't do that. I'm just bad at Spanish."

Sydney sat down and looked at her friends. She looked kind of embarrassed.

"Can you believe I ever asked Mia to join this club?" she asked in a loud voice. "I must have been crazy!"

"I'm really sorry, and I wanted you to know," I said. Then I turned and walked away. I had one more person to tell.

Jackson Montano sat at a table in a corner with a bunch of other football players. I usually never went near that table, because you always get pelted with spitballs when you walk past. But today I had to go there.

Sydney ran up behind me. "Mia, no!" she hissed. But I ignored her and walked up to him.

"Jackson, a few days ago Sydney asked me to translate that text you sent her," I said, talking fast so I wouldn't chicken out. "I thought *quiero* was *queso*, so I told her that you said she was cheesy. That's why Sydney's been spreading those rumours about you."

Jackson put down his sandwich. "Is she making you say this?"

I shook my head. "No, it's true," I said. "I should have known that *queso* was cheese."

"Yeah, you really stink at Spanish," Jackson said.

"I know," I admitted.

Jackson stared at me for a minute and glanced over at Sydney. He didn't look mad. In fact, he had a little smile on his face, as if he thought the whole thing was sort of funny. At least that's what I hoped. "I'm really, truly sorry," I said again.

Then I quickly walked away, leaving Sydney and Jackson to work things out – or not. I'm not sure what I would do if I were in Jackson's place.

When I finally made it to my regular lunch table, all my friends were staring at me.

"What was *that* all about?" Alexis asked.

I sank into my chair. "You are not going to believe this," I said, and then I told them the story.

For a moment, everybody was quiet. Then we all started laughing at the same time. Katie put her arm around Emma.

"I cheese you, Emma!" she said.

"I cheese you, too, Katie!" Emma said back.

Then Katie picked up her sandwich. "Look! My mum packed me a love sandwich for lunch."

Alexis held up the wrap on her lunch tray. "Mine's turkey and love with a little mayo."

"Really? Yum, I really cheese turkey," Katie said.

"Okay, okay!" I cried. I was laughing so hard, it was starting to hurt. "It was a colossal mistake, I know."

"So I hope you finally got a Spanish tutor," Alexis said. "You can't afford to make this kind of mistake again."

"Eddie's tutoring me, and he's actually pretty good," I said.

"Yeah, I hear he really *cheeses* tutoring Spanish," Katie said, and we collapsed into giggles.

I was embarrassed. I had no idea what kind of revenge Sydney was going to take on me. But for the first time in a long time, I felt . . . free. And pretty happy.

I grinned at my friends. "I cheese you guys so much!"

CHAPTER 15

I Figure Out Some Things

The next night Eddie helped me with my homework again, and it went really well. Eddie seemed happy.

"I knew you could do it, Mia," he said. "Keep this up and maybe you can stay in that advanced class."

"You're really good at explaining things, that's why," I said. "You should have been a teacher."

Eddie looked really pleased. "I always thought about being a teacher. Who knows? Maybe I'll give it a try someday."

As I was closing my book I heard a little ringing sound from my mobile, letting me know a text came in. I flipped open the phone and saw a message from Katie.

We're having macaroni and love for dinner
tonight. I really cheese that stuff!

I laughed out loud.

"What's so funny?" Eddie asked.

"You're not going to believe this," I said, and
then I told him the whole story.

When I was done, Eddie started to laugh, and
he didn't hold it in. Soon tears were running down
his cheeks from laughing so hard.

"Oh, that poor, poor boy," he said. "I hope you
told him what happened."

I nodded. "I did. He seems okay with it. But
I'm still worried about what Sydney will do to
me."

Eddie nodded. "No wonder, after what she did
to Jackson."

Then I found myself talking to Eddie about
Sydney — stuff I hadn't even told Mum about. Like
how Sydney wanted me to be in the PGC, but I
didn't like how she bossed everyone around. And
how she's nice to me sometimes and says insulting
things at other times.

"I agree that you shouldn't have joined her
club, but you might have hurt her feelings when
you did that," Eddie said. "Sometimes when people

are hurt, they act sad, but other people get angry and lash out."

I might have hurt Sydney's feelings? Now there was a new thought. I realised that Eddie was probably right. I had never really thought about Sydney's feelings before. I guess I figured she didn't have any.

"By the way, don't forget to ask Señora if she wants you to double-space that report that's due Friday," Eddie said as I packed up my homework.

"I don't have Spanish tomorrow because it's a half day," I said. "But you can ask her tomorrow night when you meet her."

Eddie paused. "We can ask your mum to do that," he said. "Your dad's going to go with her."

"Um, okay," I said, and I was remembering what Mum had said before about Eddie and how he should meet my teachers because he helped me with my homework. I realised now that she was right.

"And Mia?" Eddie said.

"Yeah?"

"Turn off your mobile before your mum sees you. Remember, no screens for a week."

"Oh!" I said. I had forgotten. I turned off my phone. Then I smiled at Eddie. "Thanks," I whispered, and ran up to my room. Eddie has a lot of rules, but he can also be pretty cool, I guess.

After I went up to my room, Mum came in carrying a garment bag.

"I've got another sample for you, Mia," she said. "This one's leftover from Nathan Kermit's fall line, but I think it's pretty timeless. And cute, too."

She opened the bag to reveal a really awesome blue boyfriend-style jacket with rolled-up sleeves, a plaid lining, and what looked like vintage silver buttons.

"I love it!" I exclaimed, trying it on. "I have just the shirt to go with it."

"I knew you would," Mum said, and she turned to leave.

"Hey, Mum," I said, and she stopped. "I wanted to ask you something. I think Eddie should to go the parent-teacher conference tomorrow."

Mum looked surprised. "Instead of Dad?"

I shook my head. "No, *with* Dad," I replied. "Especially since he's tutoring me in Spanish now and everything."

Mum smiled. "Let me make sure it's okay with Dad. But I'm sure he won't mind."

I hadn't even thought that Dad might be

uncomfortable being around Eddie. I guess divorce is weird for everybody involved. And it's definitely complicated! But I had a feeling that Dad would be cool with it.

The next morning I woke up feeling pretty happy about things. I was nervous about what Señora might say to my parents – all three of them – but at least everyone knew the truth now. And I got to wear my awesome new outfit.

When I got to my locker, Sydney and the PGC walked right by me.

Callie stopped. "Mia, I love your jacket," Callie said.

"Thanks," I said.

Sydney kept walking like I didn't exist, and Maggie and Bella followed her. That was just fine with me. Sydney had been totally ignoring me, but at least she wasn't telling everyone that I was going bald.

Then, on my way to registration, I passed Jackson Montano. He smiled at me, and I knew that everything was cool between us.

"Hey, Queso!" he said, teasing. But I totally didn't mind.

Since it was a half day, we all went to Alexis's house for lunch and a Cupcake Club meeting.

Alexis's dad took the day off, so he was there when we walked in the door.

"Hope you're hungry!" he called out when he heard us. "I'm making my famous grilled cheese sandwiches and tomato soup."

"Dad, that soup comes from a can," Alexis said, rolling her eyes.

"Hey, you're going to ruin my reputation," Mr Becker said. "Well, the sandwiches are all mine."

Mr Becker reminds me of Eddie sometimes. He's really friendly, and he's always joking around. We took off our coats and sat down in Alexis's neat-as-a-pin kitchen. Alexis's dad already had a bowl of soup and a sandwich at each place on the table.

"Nice service, Mr B." Katie said. "When I open up a restaurant someday, you can be a waiter."

"I'll do it if I can be *head* waiter," he said.

Katie nodded. "Deal."

We sat down to eat. The grilled cheese was crunchy on the outside and gooey on the inside, just the way I like it. Of course, Alexis opened up her notebook while we were eating.

"I have good news," she reported. "We already have three new orders based on our baker's dozen offer!"

"Woo-hoo!" Katie cheered, and we all started clapping.

Alexis told us about the orders, and we came up with some ideas. Then we just started talking about regular stuff.

"You'll never believe what Jackson Montano called me today," I said. "Queso!"

Everybody laughed.

"I guess there are worse nicknames," Emma said sympathetically.

"Anyway, I'll never forget what that word means," I said. "Plus, Eddie's tutoring is really good. He's even going to the parent-teacher conference tonight. My dad is too. That's kind of weird, isn't it?"

"It sounds kind of nice to have an extra dad," Emma said.

Katie didn't say anything. Remember how she was joking around and cheering just a minute before? Well, she was quiet for the rest of lunch. Just like before. I had a feeling I knew why, but I didn't want to bring it up in front of everybody.

Then my mobile rang, and it was Dad. (Eddie actually told Mum that I should have my phone on when I was out of the house for emergencies, and Mum totally agreed.)

"I'll be right back," I said, and walked into Alexis's living room.

"Hey, Dad," I said. "What's up?"

"I'm leaving the city now," he said. "I'll be there in plenty of time for the conference."

"Yay!" I said. Then I thought of something. "Did Mum tell you that Eddie was coming too?"

"She did," Dad replied. "It's fine with me if that's what you want, *mija*."

I had to think of a way to explain it without hurting Dad's feelings.

"Well," I began, "you're my dad, and you'll always be my dad. But when you're not here, Eddie's like a spare dad. Kind of like a baker's dozen. Most kids only get two parents. But I have three right now."

Dad laughed. "Baker's dozen, huh?"

I could hear in his voice that he was okay with that. And that was better than anything – even an extra cupcake.

CHAPTER 16

Katie Tells Me What's Wrong

$\mathcal{N}$ow that all three of my parents were going to the conference, and Dan had basketball practice, they didn't want to leave me home alone. At our school, they do the conferences over three nights. Since Katie's mum was going on Thursday, I got to hang with Katie that night.

After we ate chicken tacos and rice with Katie's mum, we went up to Katie's room. There's never a lot of homework when there's a half day, so I was showing Katie sketches I'd made of the *Emerald Forest* costumes.

"These are so cool!" Katie said, looking at a drawing of a fairy in a green sparkly dress. "You have to teach me how to sew sometime. Then we could make awesome costumes for Halloween."

"My mum's a better sewer than I am," I admitted. "Maybe she could teach both of us."

It was nice and quiet in Katie's room, with no distractions – no cupcakes, classrooms or popular girls to bother us. I figured I might as well talk to Katie about what was bothering her.

I just came right out and said it. "Are you okay?" I asked. "'Cause it seems like something's been bothering you lately. Especially when you're talking to me. And I just hope I'm not doing something to hurt your feelings or anything."

Katie didn't look at me right away. She didn't say anything right away either.

"Don't worry, it's not your fault or anything," she finally said. "It's just . . . hard to talk about, I guess."

"You can talk to me about anything," I told her. "After all, you've been hearing me complain about Mum and Dad and Eddie all the time lately. And I guess . . . I guess I thought maybe something about that was bothering you."

"Kind of," Katie admitted, turning to me. "I never see my dad. He moved away when I was a baby and has this whole other family now."

"Wow," I said. Right away I imagined what it would be like if I never saw Dad anymore. If he spent all his time with other kids, brothers and sisters I didn't even know. "That sounds awful."

"It is," Katie said. She started talking faster, like she couldn't hold in the words. "And every year I used to get a card from him at Christmas, but this year there was no card. Nothing. And it really hurts."

I felt so bad for Katie. "That's horrible."

She took a deep breath. "So when you were complaining about having *two* dads getting into your business, it kind of made me upset. I would give anything just to have one dad in my life. You're really lucky that you have two, you know?"

"I know," I said, nodding, and for the first time I really understood that I was. Having a bunch of parents can be a real pain sometimes, but it's way better than not having any. In a way, I guess I'm very lucky.

"And I know it's hard for you too," Katie told me. "It's just a different kind of situation. So I'm not mad at you at all. I'm mostly just sad for me."

"Hey, if you want, you could borrow one of my dads sometime," I said.

Katie smiled. "It all depends on how I do on my next Spanish test!"

We both laughed, and then everything felt

pretty much normal for us again. It amazes me how Katie can be such a positive person when I know how sad she must be sometimes.

I opened my sketchbook. "Let's design matching costumes for this year. You can be the Emerald Fairy, because you look fantastic in green. And I'll be the Ruby Fairy, because I look great in red."

"Wait, won't we be too old for trick-or-treating next year?" Katie asked.

"Maybe," I said. "So we'll throw a costume party! Then we'll *have* to make costumes."

Before I started sketching, my phone beeped. I jumped, thinking maybe the parent-teacher conferences were over. I was still worried about what would happen with Señora Delgado.

But it was Ava.

Avaroni: Can't wait for the party Saturday!
FabMia: Me 2! Nervous tho. Will everyone remember me?
Avaroni: RU kidding? We all miss u and can't wait to c u.
FabMia: Good!
Avaroni: How r cupcakes coming?
FabMia: We're baking them fresh for Saturday.
Avaroni: Yum!

> FabMia: Katie says hi.
> Avaroni: Hi Katie!
> FabMia: Got to go! Dad's texting.

My text conversation with Dad was much shorter.

> Your math teacher really is strict! I love all the others. Let's talk tomorrow.

"Looks like it's all over," I told Katie, after I replied to Dad. "Dad didn't say much, but it sounds like everything's all right."

"Excellent!" Katie said.

A few minutes later Mum and Eddie came to pick me up.

"How did it go?" I asked as soon as I got into the backseat.

Mum turned to talk to me. "We had a long talk with Señora Delgado. She says with the tutoring, you've been doing a lot better lately. So she's going to give you some extra assignments to help you bring up your grade."

I wasn't crazy about getting extra work, but it could have been a lot worse.

"She actually seems very nice," Eddie said. "And

I love your maths teacher, Mrs Moore. She seems like she runs a tight ship."

I shook my head and laughed. "You wouldn't like her so much if you were a student!"

It was pretty much bedtime by the time we got home. After I showered and got into my pj's, I climbed into bed and got out my sketchbook. I just wanted to finish that ruby costume before I fell asleep.

Then there was a knock on the door, and I said, "Come in!" But it wasn't Mum, as usual. It was Eddie.

"Your mum will be up in a minute," he said. "I just wanted to say that I'm glad you wanted me there tonight. I liked getting to know your teachers."

"No problem," I replied.

"Okay, then," Eddie said. "Good night, Queso!"

I groaned and pulled the covers up over my head.

See? I told you that mistake was going to haunt me forever! But like Emma said, I guess there are worse nicknames.

CHAPTER 17

Extra Good

Avaroni: Did you make my cupcakes yet?
FabMia: It's 2 early!
Avaroni: Sooooo excited!
FabMia: Me 2!
Avaroni: Wait till u see my outfit. You'll love it!
FabMia: I bet it's gorgeous. Can't wait to see u!

I yawned and rolled back over in bed. It was only eight a.m.! Ava must be really excited if she was up so early on a Saturday.

I had to get up soon anyway. We were going to make the cupcakes this morning at Emma's house, and then Eddie was going to drive me into the city so the cupcakes wouldn't get bumped around on the train.

That meant I had to pick out two different outfits – one for baking cupcakes and one for the party. What an excellent problem to have! I threw open my closet and stared at it.

Cupcake baking was easy. I pulled out my favourite pair of jeans and a long-sleeved henley top with tiny flowers on it. If I got cake mix on it, it would be easy to clean.

Then there was Ava's party. That was harder. First, I had to make sure I wore something that went with the party decorations. But also, I wanted to look extra nice. I hadn't seen some of my Manhattan friends in a long time, and I was a little nervous about it.

I changed into my cupcake clothes while I thought about the party outfit. I finally decided to wear my fuzzy white V-neck jumper with a denim skirt, boots and lots of silver jewellery. My boots are black, but the jumper and jewellery would be very snowy. I put the outfit on my bed to change into later.

After breakfast Mum took me to Emma's house, and pretty soon the Cupcake Club was busy baking. Katie and I made the cake mix, Emma made the frosting nice and fluffy and Alexis used the chopper to make the coconut like snow.

We baked two dozen, even though Ava ordered only one dozen. Most recipes make twenty-four cupcakes anyway, and this way we'd have extra if we messed up. (And Emma's brothers will always eat any leftovers we have.)

Matt came into the kitchen while we were all carefully dusting the tops of the cupcakes with coconut and edible glitter.

"More cupcakes for your boyfriends?" he asked, looking over Emma's shoulder.

"No," Emma replied firmly. "These are for a birthday party."

Matt reached to grab one, and Emma pushed his hand away.

"Not yet," she said. "We have to make them all first and pick out the best twelve for the party."

"Thirteen," Alexis corrected her. "This is Ava's first order, so she gets a baker's dozen."

Soon we had a dozen cupcakes carefully stored in a box, and one extra cupcake in a clear bag with a silver ribbon tied around it.

"Now?" Matt asked impatiently.

Emma sighed. "Now."

Matt grabbed one, unwrapped it, and then put the whole thing in his mouth.

"Good!" he said, with his mouth full.

Then Mum picked me up and brought me and the cupcakes back home. I got changed for the party, and then it was time to go into the city.

"Your chauffeur is waiting!" Eddie called up the stairs.

I ran downstairs and put on my coat. We carefully put the cupcakes in the boot, but I knew the extra one wouldn't be safe there. So I held it in my lap the whole way to the city.

There was a lot of traffic, but Eddie let me pick the music on the radio. Then, before I knew it, we were in my dad's neighbourhood.

"Call your dad and let him know we're near," he said. "I don't think I'll be able to park, so I'll drop you off in front of the building."

So I called Dad, and he was waiting outside when Eddie pulled up. He popped up the boot, and Dad moved to get my bag and the cupcakes. I was about to open the door when I thought of something.

"Thanks for all your help with Spanish," I told Eddie. I handed him the cupcake. "This is the extra baker's dozen cupcake. 'Cause you're kind of like an extra dad for me."

Eddie smiled so wide I could see every one of his teeth.

"Thanks, Mia," he said.

I quickly scooted out of the car and waved good-bye to Eddie, my extra dad. Then I ran to hug my Dad Who Will Always Be My Dad, No Matter What. It wasn't easy because he was holding the cupcakes, but I managed anyway.

I knew Ava wouldn't mind about the extra cupcake, and I was right. I got to her flat early to help set up, and she practically screamed with happiness when she saw them.

"Mia, they're beautiful!" she cried.

"Thanks. The apartment looks great!" I said.

There were little white lights, those icicle lights, strung all around the living room. Silver snowflakes hung from the ceiling. There was a long, thin table under the window for the food and stuff, and it had a white tablecloth on it with silver glitter dusted over it.

Ava looked just like a decoration herself. She wore a silver tank top with a sequin design and a fluffy white skirt, almost like the one I had drawn for her.

"Ava, you look like a snow princess!" I exclaimed.

Ava smiled and twirled around. "Mum and I looked all over for a dress, but this worked out perfectly. It really reminds me of the dress you drew for me."

By the time I had carefully set up the cupcakes on the table, the buzzer rang and the rest of the party guests started to arrive. Some of my friends from my old football team were there, like Jenny and Tamisha. Then there were friends of Ava's that I had never met before – new friends she met after I'd left. Just like my Cupcake Club friends.

I was a little nervous at first, but I fit right in. Tamisha and I were talking and laughing like we had just seen each other yesterday, and Ava's new friends were nice too.

It wasn't exactly like before, when Ava and I were best friends and I lived in Manhattan. But I was starting to think that's maybe just how life is – things keep changing, and there's nothing you can do about it. Sometimes the changes are bad, but mostly they're good, or good things can come out of them. And if something bad happens, sometimes you can learn from your mistakes and start fresh. The way my friends and I do when we make a bad batch of cupcakes.

Take right now, for example. I was having a good time at a party. I had lots of friends. I had three parents who loved me. And I wasn't failing Spanish anymore. In fact, you might say things were very good – *muy bueno*. Just don't ask me to spell that!